Jilted in January

THE RAKE REVIEW
BOOK ONE

CARA MAXWELL

Note from the Author

Throughout this book I refer to the language spoken by Edward and his family as "Chinese." This was a conscious choice because as native speakers, this is how they would have referred to their language. Given the time period, they would most likely have spoken some variation of Mandarin. I included several Mandarin words throughout the book, in their Romanized/Pinyin form. However, I also wanted to include those words in their authentic form for readers to reference. Below you will find those terms in Mandarin Chinese characters, Pinyin, and their approximate meaning in English. For more details, please read the Author's Note at the end of the book.

心肝 Xīngān = darling
奶奶 nǎi nai = paternal grandmother
爸爸 Bàba (Bà) = informal father
妈妈 Māmā (Mā) = informal mother

Chapter One

Mayfair, London
January 1820

I f the devil himself had looked inside of Edward Johns' mind and designed a corner of hell just for him, it would have been this ballroom.

At age eleven, he'd thought hell was the icy water of Portsmouth, where he'd nearly drowned after following his father down to the docks without permission.

At twenty and one, he'd have sworn it was on a ship bound for the West Indies, where he hung over the rail retching his guts into the sea while the crewmen exchanged laughs and bets on whether the boss' son would last the week.

But at nearly thirty, Edward had refined his notions of heaven and hell. Hell was standing at the edge of a ballroom, ignoring progressively blatant advances from the most delectable women the *ton* had to offer, contemplating how he was going to extricate his younger brother from his latest disaster.

Not a ringing endorsement for the first ball of the Season.

He knocked back the ratafia, refusing to let himself cringe. It had taken years, but he'd mastered that particular impulse. He mastered everything eventually. Self-control was the only way to survive in London.

It was the only way for *Edward Johns* to survive in London.

Lords had it easy.

The Duke of Exeter, who was holding court a few yards away, did not need to concern himself with perfect decorum. That wastrel spent half of his life foxed, making no attempt to better himself as he searched for an heiress to save his beleaguered dukedom. What self-control did he need, when he had the power to make a duchess out of a mere miss?

And the brown-haired bloke that stood at the duke's side, the Marquess of Clydon, all raffish grins and effusive laughter and inappropriately heated looks at his gregarious blonde wife? He could do whatever he damn well pleased, and stuff the consequences. The *ton* would love him no matter what.

But it had no such affection for Edward.

Never had.

Never would.

His father might be perfectly respectable, the grandson of a duke. But taking a Chinese wife was hardly more excusable now than it had been thirty years prior when the elder Mr. Johns had done it.

It had taken him ten long years, becoming rich enough to rival the King himself, for Edward to earn acceptance in the ballrooms of the *ton*. He'd made peace with the fact that he'd always be on the outskirts, allowed in these gilded ballrooms because of his money and his usefulness.

And usually, it did not bother him. He was more than happy to take one beautiful widow after another to his bed. But tonight he had a purpose—one that every wicked widow or dissatisfied dame seemed intent on keeping him from.

None more determined than Lady Pelham, who approached from the left, slipping through the crowd in a wispy silver gown.

She was a bit thinner than he preferred, but fresh out of mourning for a husband who had been thirty years her senior meant she'd be enthusiastic in the bedroom.

However, he'd no sooner sighted Lady Pelham when he noticed Mrs. Angelica Weston edging around the dance floor with two glasses of ratafia in her hand. Since her husband had taken ship to Virginia to oversee his holdings, she'd been systematically working her way through the rakes of the *ton*.

God, save me.

Two very tempting offers for the night. And yet, he could not pursue either of them.

Hell.

On any other night, he would have smiled at them. Accepted the ratafia. Tilted his head toward the balcony in silent invitation. But tonight he could not afford to be the rake that London society had made him, because his younger brother was missing.

Again.

He set aside the empty glass and cut a line through the crowd in the opposite direction of the ladies Pelham and Weston. The Fixer was there. Now he needed to find her.

In moonlit night, a rose so fair, whispers frosty tales, beyond compare.

He'd paid a pound sterling for that single line—the line that would allow him to recognize the Fixer. The lady who knew everything about the ton. Hopefully, the one who would be able to help him find his brother, Alfred.

His hand dropped into the pocket of his tailcoat. His fingers scraped along the edge of the carefully folded paper. He'd hesitated to fold it, afraid that might somehow interfere with the note's integrity. As if a folded edge would somehow hamper the Fixer in determining the note's provenance.

The ransom note had appeared on his desk three days earlier, which was three days after he'd gone to Alfred's residence in Limehouse only to find it deserted. For those first three days, he'd searched Alfred's usual haunts. For the last three, he'd been deciding whether to leave his brother to this supposed ransom or hire an investigator.

He doubted that Alfred was truly in any danger. This was just the sort of scheme his brother and his mates would make up for a jape. But he did need to find the wastrel before their parents realized he was missing.

Which was how he'd arrived in this particular hell. Attending a ball, which he abhorred. Avoiding the women who would have made the ball bearable. And searching for a woman called The Fixer, with nothing more than a few lines of poetry to direct him.

Edward pulled his hand out of his pocket a half-second before it curled into a fist, just short of crushing the note that was his only lead to finding his younger brother.

A rose so fair.

That was simple enough. He knew the Fixer was a woman, so the woman would be wearing a rose. Or was the mention of the rose an allusion to the fact that the Fixer was female? An English rose.

Shit.

He scanned the crowd as he walked, dodging more than one lustful glance.

In moonlit night...

Would she be out on the balcony? It was frigid out there, but it was as good a place to start as any.

Edward nodded to the Earl of Bravern. He had no friends among the *ton*, but Bravern had always been cordial. But Edward did not stop to talk. He darted his gaze away before there could be any sort of invitation, slipping out into the hallway, then through the tightly closed doors...

To find nothing.

No one.

The balcony was deserted.

Of course it was.

It was January, there was a thin layer of snow on the ground, and not a single inch of the moon was visible through the thick layer of clouds overhead.

He stomped back inside, hardly noticing the flush of warmth as he reentered the ballroom. The lords were as brightly dressed as the ladies, despite the cold air outside. As if the members of the ton were determined to defy the frigid winter by dressing in bright pinks and yellows. One dandy even wore a ridiculous bright green striped tailcoat.

One of the few dressed with any sort of sense was a woman on the other side of the dance floor, her back to him as she spoke with a knot of other women.

There was something eerily familiar about the tilt of her head.

She wore deep sapphire blue. The color of the ocean, but not during the day. The taffeta shimmered slightly as she moved, reminiscent of the nights he'd spent at sea, when the moonlight would gild the sky and waves.

In moonlit night, a rose so fair...

There was a white rose in her hair, pinned up with the dark curls.

A white rose in the middle of winter. She must know someone with a hothouse.

A pang of warning—Edward ignored it. He'd finally found her, the Fixer who would help him find his brother, who could finally put an end to the awful night.

He darted through the crowd, then pulled himself back, forcing himself to slow, to move at a reasonable pace. He shouldn't draw attention to himself. No more than he normally did just by existing as an interloper in these august halls.

He'd need an introduction, he reminded himself. He could not simply walk up to a woman he'd never met and start demanding that she assist him. He had to follow all of society's rules, always. First, he had to get a good look at her. See who she was speaking with. Ascertain her identity, and then deduce who in the ballroom could and would provide him with an introduction.

Edward angled himself wide, skirting dangerously close to the dance floor. Mere proximity to all that swirling made him anxious. But he forced himself onward.

He descended into the place inside of him that was all control, all calm calculation. Descended too far, because his body ricocheted off of someone else's. A woman. Tall. Coltish. Not a face he recognized, even as her eyes went big and round. *She* recognized *him*.

But he didn't have time to feel anything about that.

"I beg your pardon!" he tossed over his shoulder, not even really looking at the poor woman.

He was much too focused, too fixated on the woman just ahead. The crowd was parting, and—

Shit.

Edward knew those dark curls, artfully arranged to fall over her shoulders and frame her face. He recognized the pale skin, the round face, the trio of freckles that formed a perfect line down the column of her throat.

He didn't need an introduction.

He needed a miracle.

Edward thought himself in hell? The devil certainly did have a sense of humor.

After what he'd done ten years ago, getting Persephone Cuthbert to speak to him again would take an act of God.

Chapter Two

S even years, and London hadn't changed a whit.

Yes, the fashions were slightly different. Prinny was in charge. Most of her friends were married with children. But the swirling eddies of gossip were the same, as were most of the faces, if a bit aged.

Most importantly, she'd already been covertly approached by two women seeking her services.

A shiver of excitement snaked down Persephone's spine.

She'd been worried that her reputation as the Lady Fixer of New York would not follow her home to London. But the seeds she had planted at the house parties she'd attended in November and December had sprouted with gratifying efficiency.

Miss Anna Winlock's favorite reticule had gone missing during her elder sister's at-home last week.

Lady Olivia St. James worried her youngest son was secretly maintaining a mistress.

She'd have both of their queries sorted within a fortnight.

Her fingers curled with need, eager to pull her small notebook from her reticule and begin jotting notes. But now was not the time to descend into her intricate configurations of arrows and words, flowing together and apart and making sense of even the most complex tasks.

Now she had a different part to play—the brilliant duke's daughter, freshly returned from America, eager to find a husband and do her duty.

Except that it wasn't going quite as well as she'd hoped.

She was renewing acquaintances, chatting eagerly with the young women who had been her friends when she made her debut all those seasons ago.

But only two gentlemen had asked her to dance. A poor showing.

Persephone had returned to London with two goals—to carve out a niche for herself just as she had done in New York, stimulating her ever-hungry mind; and to find a husband.

She'd been so focused on the first, she'd neglected the second and slightly less important of her two endeavors. *Equally important,* she amended. She was twenty-seven years old. A spinster, by most accounts. She'd anticipated that it might be difficult to catch the attention of the gentleman of the *ton,* with so many debutantes for competition.

But Persephone was the daughter of a duke. She had a dowry to dwarf all others. She'd thought that having newly returned from seven years in New York would make her interesting and alluring.

Instead, the fact that she'd returned to London without a husband just made her look inadequate.

She was determined not to let it bother her. If she set herself to the task of finding a husband with the same temerity as she did her hired tasks, she'd succeed. She always succeeded. Every reticule found. Every wayward son's affairs uncovered.

Persephone was very good at getting what she wanted.

And she was careful only to want things she could actually get.

She'd learned that lesson the painful way.

"I do not see the Duke and Duchess. Are they with you this evening?" the woman beside her asked politely.

Lady Mary Harmon was exactly that—perfectly, primly, agonizingly polite. She'd been the perfect debutante a decade before, and now she was the perfect matron, wife, and mother. Persephone smiled at the smaller woman—because really, how could she not at someone so sweet?

"They've missed my return, unfortunately. My father cancelled his grand tour when he was young, assuming the dukedom so suddenly. My mother has been needling him for years to make up for it." A hint of sadness, that was all Persephone allowed herself. She hadn't seen her parents in nearly three years, since their last visit to New York.

They'd be home in a few months.

Hopefully by then, she'd have an engagement to share with them.

"What a shame," Mary said. The perfectly polite response.

Persephone couldn't help her gaze drifting, scanning over the crowded ballroom as she looked for more faces she'd recognize.

"Who is hosting you—"

"*No.*" She grabbed Mary's arm without thinking.

"I beg your pardon... Lady Persephone, are you well? You look like you've—AH!" Mary broke off with a squeak.

Persephone flinched, quickly releasing the other woman. Mary rubbed at the ache where Persephone's hand had been moments before.

"I am so very sorry, I was surprised." Surprised was the mildest word. Mortified. Flabbergasted. Those were more accurate. "I thought I saw a friend from New York. But I was mistaken."

Persephone forced herself to take a breath, to look back at Mary and resume a normal conversation.

But the other woman had already followed her gaze. Right to Edward Johns.

Persephone was either going to retch or swoon. Or maybe,

just maybe, the anger that burned inside of her would explode outward and she'd be consumed by a living flame. Hopefully she would take Edward down with her.

He deserved no less.

"Are you acquainted with Mr. Johns?" Mary asked, voice no more than a squeak.

"Unfortunately," Persephone said under her breath. "Come, let us find some refreshment." She looped her arm through the other woman's and started to steer her through the crowd. Of course, Mary did not complain. *Too polite.*

Persephone sent up a silent prayer of thanks.

They made their way to the refreshment table and Persephone dipped two tumblers of ratafia. She slid her gaze casually behind them as she lifted the glass to her lips.

Heavens above, he was cutting through the crowd.

Edward Johns was rushing straight toward her.

The ratafia sloshed out of the glass—Heavens above! Her hand was shaking!—nearly hitting her sapphire blue skirts. Mary's eyes widened, but Persephone didn't have time to come up with something clever.

"Excuse me, I'm a bit dizzy. I believe I need to lie down." She shoved the glass into the other woman's hand.

Mary took the glass without argument. "Of course..."

But if she said more, Persephone didn't hear it. She was already in the hall, just short of running.

She'd dissect the irony of running away from Edward Johns later on. When she was safe back in her bedroom at the Marchioness of Clydon's mansion. When she was protected by walls and her chaperones from the man who had unceremoniously broken her heart. When he wasn't—

Standing right in front of her.

Blocking her path.

As if he'd anticipated exactly where she was going.

He crossed his arms over his chest and lifted his chin a fraction of an inch. The way that he did when he was getting ready to win an argument. Heavens, she wished she didn't know that.

Just like she wished she didn't know that he had a dimple hiding in that stern left cheek. Or how his lips felt against hers.

"You cannot avoid me all night," he said matter-of-factly.

"Yes, I can," she bit out, sharp and reactive.

The scent of bergamot and anise accosted her. How insufferable of him to still be using the same exact soap he'd used a decade ago. How infuriating that he dared to get close enough to her that she could even smell it.

She was three yards from the ladies' retiring room. He would not follow her there, she felt certain. She darted for the door.

Edward grabbed her hand and dragged her back. "Persephone—"

"Lady Persephone!" She ripped her hand back. Tried to. But the blasted man had always been unnervingly strong.

"You do not get to call me by my given name," she said sharply, yanking again. To no avail.

His dark eyes flashed. His precious self-control wavering, just for a second. A decade ago, she would have grinned in triumph and then covered his smirking mouth with a kiss. Now, she just wanted to slap him.

"Lady Persephone," Edward said, still holding her hand tight. Heavens, it sounded all wrong. And her name on his tongue had sounded so right.

She was supposed to be over this, over him. She *was* over him.

There was a slight tick in his jaw, but he maintained the resolute angle of his chin. "I need to speak with you privately."

Persephone gave him the most scathing glare she could manage. "You do not get to do that, either."

A slow inhale. "I need your help."

"Too damn bad," she said reflexively, hardly even processing what he'd said.

He blinked—surprise. It was enough for Persephone to

wrench her arm away. She darted off in the other direction, away from the retiring room. Edward Johns was stubborn enough to stand outside of it all night, waiting for her to come back out. Her only recourse was to leave the ball entirely. It was a disappointing end to the evening, but it would allow her time to start on the tasks she'd accepted and to reassess her approach to husband-hunting. She'd hoped that a few more clients might have found her that night, but given the secretive nature of her work it was possible that they simply had not had time to work out the riddle.

There had to be some pretense of secrecy, or she'd never be able to accomplish her tasks while avoiding embarrassment for her clients. But perhaps she needed a different method for helping the women of the *ton* identify her.

Another thing she'd think about once she was safely away from Edward, the man she'd hoped never to see again.

But she could feel him right behind her. Reaching for her shoulder, missing as she dashed forward. Her foot caught on the threshold, she nearly careened forward onto the dance floor—but Edward reached for her again. He caught her on the shoulder, pulling her back with enough force that she fell back against him, her spine fitting in against his broad chest with startling ease.

The heat rising in her stomach was the least of her problems just then.

The entire ballroom could see them now. No escape.

Persephone plastered a smile to her face, inclining her head. "Dance with me."

The choking sound that came out of Edward's throat was almost vindicating enough to make the entire painful interaction worth it.

"I do not dance," he said, his deep voice grating over the syllables.

Persephone refused to remember how that same rough timbre had sounded when he moaned against her skin.

"If you wish to speak with me privately, then ask me to

dance." She glanced over her shoulder, lifting her chin to accentuate the curve of her throat. Edward had always had such a weakness for her throat.

His eyes darted over her mouth, then lower.

Sweet, sweet vindication.

There was no way that Edward would give up a lifelong abhorrence for something so trivial as speaking to her, she assured herself.

"Fine."

He grabbed her hand and blast it, but her feet moved of their own accord. The music was starting. His hand was around her waist—they were dancing!

She was dancing with Edward Johns.

Now Persephone actually did think she might swoon.

She'd been in uncomfortable situations like this before, she reminded herself. She was the Lady Fixer. She *put* herself in these sorts of situations to complete tasks. Edward was another task, another thing to be lived through and then checked off of her mental list.

Except that his hand on her waist was sending waves of heat through her body.

Anger.

It was anger.

It couldn't possibly be attraction. Not after all these years.

She picked a spot on the wall of the ballroom, just as she had when she'd first learned to dance and got dizzy from spinning. No matter how she turned and twirled, she returned her gaze to that spot. Tried to anchor herself.

But there was a tall, slender lady standing just below the spot she'd picked. Despite her attempts to concentrate, it was impossible to miss the scathing look the woman sent in their direction.

Edward's direction.

She ought to bite down on her tongue and ignore it. The sooner this dance was over, the sooner she would be free of him once again. But, of course, she couldn't resist a problem that needed solving. "Why is that young woman glaring at you?"

Edward's mouth hung open—he'd been about to speak. Instead, his eyes darted around, searching. "How am I supposed to—oh. The one over by the wall?"

"Yes."

His chin dipped a tiny bit. "I may have knocked into her in my haste to make your acquaintance."

"Charming as ever." The irony was bitter in her throat. He had been charming, once. Before he ripped her heart out of her chest, stomped on it, and proceeded to bed half of the ladies of the *ton*.

Edward was not a problem to be solved. He was heartbreak wrapped in handsome and she needed to get him away from her as quickly as possible.

"What is it you want?" she said.

His dark eyes flicked back to her, focusing with an intensity that told Persephone as much as his words. Whatever this was about, it was important.

"I am trying to find someone. I have a ransom note which I would like you to look at. That is all."

She blinked. Once, twice. Dodged his foot. A decade had not improved his dancing skills.

It was so perfectly succinct and factual. So very Edward.

As if a disappearance and a ransom note were perfectly normal things to discuss on the dance floor. It was no wonder he'd wanted to speak privately. But why her...

Understanding dawned, painful and sharp.

She'd done an even better job at seeding her reputation than she'd realized. He'd seen the white rose in her hair, had recognized the sapphire gown from her riddle.

She swallowed carefully, ignoring the way Edward's eyes dipped to her throat. "I do not usually deal with things of this... nature."

His dark eyes jumped up to hers. "They call you the Fixer."

"In New York they called me the *Lady* Fixer. A favorite vase goes missing. A maid having a tryst with the second son. That sort of thing." She hated that it sounded as if she was minimizing her accomplishments. But if it got Edward to let her be and disappear from her life once again, then so be it.

His jaw was ticking again, and something like resignation shadowed his eyes. "You are not up to it."

And there was the fire once again.

Her hand tightened on his arm. "That is not what I said."

She needed to stop talking. She did not want to help him. She wanted him as far away from her as possible. Preferably on another continent. If that was no longer feasible—she doubted he'd be leaving his father's shipping company now that he'd made himself as rich as Croesus—then at least in a different building was the bare minimum.

Edward's hold on her only tightened. That damned scent was flooding her senses, reminding her of stolen nights she'd thought long forgotten.

"Alfred has been missing for six days—"

"Alfred?!" she gasped. Sweet, kind Alfred?

She remembered Edward's younger brother perfectly. The cherubic round face, the pin-straight black hair that fell into his eyes, the way he seemed to bounce from room to room. He must be... nineteen years old?

And disappeared. Kidnapped, if a ransom note was involved.

"Give me the note," she demanded.

Edward drew back sharply. "No."

"No?" Persephone hissed. There were too many people watching to do what she really wanted—to stomp on his foot or bring her knee up hard between his legs.

Once, she'd allowed Edward to make an utter fool of her.

But Persephone would be damned if she let him make one of her again.

"You chased me across this ball, embarrassed us both, and now you are tromping all over my feet. And you don't want my help?" she asked sharply.

Edward did not even bother to look stricken as he corrected her. "I did not say that."

"You said you will not give me the note," Persephone said. She tried to pull herself out of his grip. Tried very hard not to notice the thick muscles she could feel beneath her hands or the comforting way his body seemed to enclose hers.

Comforting? She was losing her mind and she'd only been with the man a few minutes. She could not help him. She would refuse his task. Not because the Lady Fixer was not capable of it. But because she was likely to end up wanted for murder if she did.

Edward dipped his head closer so she could hear him closer over the rising music. "Not here."

"Then when?" she heard herself asking. *Why was she asking?* She was not going to help him. Blast her, she wanted to help Alfred. Sweet, kind Alfred, who had never said a cruel word to her. Unlike the man whose arms she was currently dancing in.

"I will call on you," Edward said.

"You do not even know where I am staying," she scoffed. The set was almost over. She was nearly free. "And I am not going to tell you. You don't know anything about me. Not anymore. You must find someone else to help you. This is entirely inappropriate."

Edward stared at her with an inscrutable expression that not even the Lady Fixer could read.

"You are correct, of course, Lady Persephone. I should not have presumed," he finally said, all careful politeness.

Now that she'd decreed she would not help him, and he'd apparently accepted it, he could just banish the emotions.

How nice that must be.

The dance was ending. She only had a few seconds.

Persephone dove into her spinning mind, searching for some

witty retort that would somehow repay Edward for ten years of pain.

But he was already stepping away, bowing, taking a half step back toward the crowd.

He melted back into the throng, easily blending in with the taller gentlemen until she couldn't see him at all.

Just like that, he'd dismissed her.

It should have made her happy. Ten years ago, she'd vowed she never wanted to lay eyes on Edward Johns ever again. She'd crossed an ocean to get away from him.

So why did it feel like she should be running after him?

Chapter Three

Dearest reader,

Is there anything quite as bracing as the kiss of cold air on your cheeks as you step out of the carriage and into the thrall of the first ball of the season? A real kiss, perhaps?

Of course, many a lady knows exactly the taste and tannin of a kiss from Mr. E__ J__. This dashing rake has turned the head of as many ladies as there are ships bearing his father's name.
I doubt I need to mention the shipping empire he stands to inherit, but what about his proclivity for spoiling his conquests with shiny trinkets? Rumor has it that he is as skilled in a hammock as he is in a four-poster. Though the lady that mentioned that particular tidbit shall remain anonymous.

But then, all women are but another forgettable distraction to an unreformed rake like Mr. E__ J__. It does not stop the ladies of London from seeking his company. Who could resist that broad chest and those finely-honed muscles made for climbing rigging... or into his next paramour's bed.

Alas, our beloved wanton widows may have to look elsewhere for someone to keep them warm on these bitter winter nights, for the unthinkable has finally happened. Mr. E__ J__ was spotted twirling around the dance floor!

If you can manage to drag your jaw up from the floor—this brazen belle certainly struggled to—then you deserve to know that he partnered with none other than the newly returned to London Lady P__ C__. What could have enticed our dance-abhorring dandy to go back on a decade's worth of stalwart refusals and join the melee? Does Lady P__ C__ know something we do not?

One thing is for certain, dear readers. The most unmarriageable man in London has just gotten even more interesting.

No matter what happens with Mr. E__ J___, this writer shall return next month. There are far too many scoundrels in London these days to settle for raking just one of them over the coals.

Your bold and brazen friend,

The Belle

* * *

Persephone let the scandal sheet drop to the polished mahogany table.

On any other morning, it would have been funny. If there had been any names mentioned other than her and Edward.

The Brazen Belle.

Persephone didn't know if she wanted to strangle the gossip columnist or applaud her. She did know that once the ladies of the *ton* got ahold of this column, Edward's entire life would change. By declaring him the most unmarriageable man in

London, the Belle had ensured that every eye would be on him. Every matchmaking mama would be wondering if perhaps they'd misjudged him, if it had been a mistake to overlook the fortune in ships anchored in ports across England. Every debutante would be reminded of just how broad those shoulders of his were. And the experienced widows looking for company...

Her stomach rolled traitorously.

But before she could even begin to analyze *why*, the door to the dining room opened and a whirlwind with bright golden hair spun into the room.

"Mother, I must speak to you!"

Madison Warsham slowly set down the newssheet she'd been reading in her seat, directly across the table from Persephone. She was about halfway through the stack in front of her. When she'd first arrived in London, Persephone had thought it a rather strange habit, reading every newssheet every single day. The Marchioness of Clydon even had them delivered from farther abroad—Southampton, York. They may be a day or two delayed by the time they arrived, but she consumed them with the same diligence she did the fresh periodicals from London proper.

Persephone wasn't inclined to question her friend turned chaperone for the season. With her parents away on the Continent and Madison as her host, she had a considerable amount of freedom.

Besides, Madison also had the scandal sheets brought in with the news—which were infinitely more useful to Persephone in pursuit of her tasks.

Except when her name was sprawled across them.

If only the Brazen Belle knew that they'd spent the entire dance bickering like children. At least then, the ladies of the ton would not be fooled into thinking Edward was some prize to be won.

On the other side of the table, Madison turned her attention to the child bouncing on her toes a few feet inside the door.

Madison inclined her head, her long blonde hair catching the morning light and gleaming as brightly as her daughter's.

"Must you? How very dire it sounds," Madison said, her lips curving.

The little girl's eyes flickered.

Persephone bit her lip to keep in her chuckle.

"Come, sit beside me, Nora." Madison patted the empty chair at her side.

The child hazarded a glance in Persephone's direction, but did as her mother said.

The first time that Persephone had seen her old friend with a child, it had seemed odd. But the more time she spent in their company, the more normal it became. Comforting, even, to see the sweet interactions between the little family.

Nora wiggled into the seat, folding her hands carefully in her lap as she met her mother's expectant gaze. "Nurse says that I must take my daily constitutional. But it is so cold. I can see my breath!"

Madison merely sipped her tea and waited for the five-year-old to continue. An experienced mother, already.

"I ought to stay in and read," Nora said, her voice gaining confidence. "I've almost finished the book Father brought me about the Roman conquest of Britain."

Madison tilted her head to the side, as if seriously considering her daughter's predicament. Persephone bit even harder into her lip.

"If I recall, you have an hour for reading directly after your walk," Madison said.

Nora jumped to her feet, protest already upon her lips, but the door to the dining room opened once again.

The Marquess of Clydon strode in, all long, tall planes and wide smiles for his wife, daughter, and their guest.

"Papa!" Nora squealed, springing after him. "I want to stay in and read."

"Of course, you do." He dropped a kiss to her golden head, then another, longer one on his wife's before settling into the seat at the head of the table. He crossed his long legs and grinned at his daughter, his cheeks still reddened from his morning shave.

"What are you reading?" he asked little Nora.

"That is immaterial, Henry," Madison cut in.

The Marquess ducked his head. This time, Persephone let her soft laugh escape. Henry Warsham might tower over his wife in physical stature, but Madison's force of personality filled the room.

Still south of thirty, she was one of the *ton's* most sought-after hostesses—if also one of its most controversial.

Madison speared her husband a cowing scowl before turning back to their daughter. "Darling, you must not come calling to your father and I every time Nurse makes a decision you dislike. It is not kind."

The girl's eyes widened, but she nodded. "Yes, Mother."

"Come now, sit in my lap and we'll read the next newssheet together before you go. This one mentions the Princess of Wales." Before the words had even fully left Madison's lips, Nora was scrambling into her mother's lap, settling her head back against her shoulder so their matching golden hair mingled together.

Henry made a soft sound of appreciation from the other end of the table as he dug into his breakfast.

Persephone's heart stuck in her throat.

This is what I want.

She had always known she wanted children, but it was more than that. She wanted a family. It was too much to ask for a love match like Henry and Madison, of course. People still whispered about the pair of them, even all these years later.

But she'd be perfectly satisfied with comfortable respect and affection. A husband who could give her that, and children, while still allowing her to complete her tasks as the Lady Fixer of London. It wasn't too much to hope for, was it?

You are not up to it.

Edward's words echoed in her head. As cruel as ever, it seemed. Even ten years later.

But that did not mean his younger brother, Alfred, should have to suffer.

Her eyes snagged on the scandal sheet, forgotten in front of her as she'd enjoyed the familial tableau her hosts so effortlessly presented.

This time, her stomach didn't turn over. Instead, her lips curved into a small smile.

She folded it carefully, slipping it into the pocket of her gown without the slightest bit of notice from the trio across the table. Then she took a sip of her tea, her smile widening. "I think I shall join you for your walk, Nora."

Chapter Four

Walking away from Persephone had been the most profound sort of torture.

Ten years ago, he'd said goodbye. Among many other cruel and hurtful things, to try and convince the love of his life that she had no future with him, that there was no hope for reconciliation. It had felt like ripping his heart out of his own chest, but Edward had been able to do it because he knew it was the best thing for Persephone.

But walking away from her at the ball the night before? That had been nigh on impossible. He'd made a complete muddle of things. Once he'd seen her across that ballroom and realized she was the Fixer he sought, his brain had stopped working properly.

First, he'd inadvertently insulted her abilities as the Lady Fixer. Then, when she'd asked to see the note, indicating she might actually be willing to help him, he'd told her no. His instant reaction was to keep her far, far away from whatever mess Alfred had entangled himself with.

But it might be perfect.

Shit.

He was running out of time.

The ransom note was painfully specific. Date, time, location, and how much money he needed to bring if he ever wanted to see Alfred alive again.

Edward doubted the scheme would actually end in Alfred's death. His brother was reckless, but never quite that reckless. The most likely scenario was that he'd overextended himself at the card table, and his gambling mates were using the ransom scheme to extract the money he owed them.

They were probably comfortably ensconced in a room at one of myriad gentleman's clubs in Mayfair, drinking away the days until the ransom was due.

Like hell was Edward going to give his hard-earned money away to Alfred's idiot mates.

But it might be the perfect opportunity...

He shook his head to clear the thought. Apparently, his mind still had not resumed normal function since his encounter with Persephone.

Being trapped inside was not helping.

Edward preferred the dockside, the small apartment he kept above his father's warehouse more than sufficient for his needs. But Alfred had been taken from just such an apartment in Limehouse. It seemed prudent to relocate, if only temporarily. Even if he suspected that the whole scenario was a jape.

But while his suite at the Pendleton in Mayfair boasted every possible amenity his money could buy, it lacked the briny saltwater air and sense of self-determination that always came from hard, honest work.

Nothing about the nobility in London was hard-working or honest.

Edward pulled the greatcoat tighter over his chest as he walked, dodging the eyes of the patrons assembled in the Pendleton's reception area.

Were there more of them than usual? He reached for his pocket watch to check the time, then stilled the impulse. Eyes forward, chin high. Any twitch would be perceived as a weakness.

Much had changed in the ten years since Persephone's departure from his life. But the need to be perfect? That had only solidified.

Ten years spent building a fortune and earning invitations to increasingly more illustrious social gatherings. Edward was wealthier than Midas, having taken a third interest in his father's shipping company six years ago. He had cultivated relationships with the prosperous lords of the *ton*, enticing them to invest in shipping cargoes that made them and him richer, year over year.

Through his unbridled determination, the *ton* had accepted him. As much as it ever would an untitled, half-Chinese man. But one mistake, and that reputation would career back into the gutter.

He made it to the street, ready to dodge across between two carriages. He was fast enough to avoid the churning wheels and hooves.

"Good day, Mr. Johns. Do you require transportation this morning?"

Edward bit down hard on the inside of his cheek. "No," he said to the liveried footman standing at the hotel door. Then begrudgingly added, "Thank you."

The man bobbed his chin. "Enjoy your day, Mr. Johns."

But the crisp words were cushioned with softer, more muffled ones.

Were those whispers?

Edward jerked his head to the side. A knot of patrons was alighting from a carriage on the hotel's doorstep. The eldest woman leaned over, speaking in a quick, indecipherable mutter to the younger woman at her side. They didn't even try to avert their eyes as he discovered them watching him brazenly.

His hands, already curled tightly at his side from the restrained tension of too many hours spent indoors, loosened.

Edward was used to the staring.

There had only ever been one person who looked at him and did not see his heritage. Or rather, who saw that heritage and admired it, rather than scoffing.

But when she'd seen him the night before, she'd recoiled just the same. And that had nothing to do with his parentage and everything to do with the fact that he'd broken her heart. At least the ire she sent in his direction was deserved.

Seeing her had been like cutting open a wound that was nearly healed. Except that it never had, not really. *That* had become painfully clear the instant he took her in his arms on that dance floor.

The last ten years had been a waste.

He'd built a fortune, fortified his father's empire, gained the tenuous acceptance of the ton. But his heart... that had been woefully neglected.

No woman he'd met in those storied drawing rooms had ever touched that place inside of him.

If the ladies of the *ton* looked at him like an oddity, an exotic novelty to gossip about with their friends... at least fucking them temporarily filled the hole inside of him. The one left behind by—

"Persephone!" Edward pulled himself up just short of mowing her over. He'd been too busy lost in memory. He cleared his throat, shaking out his fisted hands once again.

She looked... perfect. Damn it all.

Her wild dark curls were tamed beneath a pale blue cap, trimmed in sapphire ribbon that framed her face and made her dark eyes stand out against her creamy pale skin. He didn't dare let his gaze wander past her face. Noticing how carefully the sky-blue wool of her pelisse was molded to her body? That would be a mistake.

Her face was safer. Even if it was unfairly lovely in the cold January air.

"Lady Persephone," he corrected himself, voice even and controlled once more. If a bit demanding as he added, "What are you doing here?"

Hell and damnation. He could keep a leash on his tongue around everyone but her.

Persephone pursed her lips, one full lip stacking atop the other in an expression that effortlessly communicated her annoyance. Then her mouth smoothed out, curving softly into a smile that made Edward even more nervous.

She was up to something.

"The Pendleton is a fashionable place to take afternoon tea," she said, lifting her chin. Giving him a view of her throat, left exposed by the open top button of her pelisse.

It was too cold for the choice to have been anything but deliberate.

Edward was not the only one who'd been ruminating in memories.

He let the scowl that he'd normally have suppressed play across his face, if only to give him a moment to think. *Why was she seeking him out when she wanted nothing to do with him or finding his brother?* "You are not here to take tea."

A statement, not a question. One that Persephone didn't attempt to refute.

She merely shrugged her delicate shoulders, glancing around at the group of patrons that had been watching him so closely, now moving inside the warmth of the hotel. Even gossip couldn't keep out the frigid January wind.

"You haven't received any extra attention this morning?" she asked, dark brown eyes still lingering on their retreating backs.

Maybe she recognized them.

Maybe one of the ladies had come to her to *fix* a problem.

He certainly wasn't trying to draw her eyes back to him by saying, "I always receive extra attention."

There went her lips again. "Do not be crude."

Edward liked the pursed pout more than the fake smile anyway. "I was referencing my parentage, not my nocturnal activities."

As soon as he said it, he wished he hadn't. The last thing he wanted to discuss with Persephone was the string of women he'd bedded in the ten years since their engagement had ended.

But Persephone's cheeks had flushed pink to match her pouting lips. "From what I hear, they are far from confined to the night."

Hell and damnation. Were they really having this conversation?

"You wish to talk about my amorous exploits?" he asked incredulously.

Less than five minutes in her presence, and his calm exterior was shattered. Ten years, and it hadn't cracked once. Not a single scathing look nor a night of passion had done to him what she could effortlessly do in a few minutes' time.

What was worse was that aside from the pink of her cheeks, which could easily be explained away by the cold, she looked entirely unbothered. As if she *would* continue discussing the dozens of women he'd bedded since leaving her, and not care one fig.

She lifted one gloved hand to gesture across the street, where a small park covered in frost stood silent and empty. "Shall we walk?"

"Shall you tell me why you're haunting my steps when last night you looked like you'd rather drown me than talk to me?" He could not help it, he realized. They had always challenged each other, teased. Falling back into it was as natural as breathing. Except for Persephone, the barbs were real.

But she was already halfway across the street, dodging half-frozen mud puddles and not even bothering to glance behind her. She knew he would follow.

The miniscule park was a meagre imitation of the briny

freedom of the docks. But with Persephone and him walking the paths, it was guaranteed to be salty.

She paused on the other side of the street, waiting until he was abreast of her, but only just, to speak again.

"I came here as a courtesy," she said with unbridled alacrity.

Before he could ask what the hell that meant, her hand darted into the angular stitched pocket of her pelisse. She withdrew a neatly folded square and offered it to him.

The slight smirk lurking just beneath her façade was enough to have him recoiling from the folded paper. "What is it?"

Persephone slid a gloved finger underneath the seam, flipping the paper open.

"It was delivered to every noble house in London this morning," she said, holding it up a little higher. So that even if he didn't take it from her, he couldn't avoid reading a few of the words.

The Rake Review.

What bit of composure he'd kept intact dropped away, dissolved by the acid in his stomach as his eyes read line after line of the scandal sheet.

Rumor has it that he is as skilled in a hammock...

Does Lady P__ C__ know something...

The most unmarriageable man in London has just gotten even more interesting...

Calm composure? He was going to combust on the spot.

Being targeted by a gossip column was precisely the sort of scandal he worked so hard to avoid. Some of the lords and ladies enjoyed having the eyes of the *ton* on them, basking in the momentary fame. But more eyes meant more opportunities for someone to find fault with him. He needed to find Alfred, and this would only complicate matters.

He ripped the scandal sheet out of Persephone's hand. "This is libel. I will—"

"What will you do, Edward? Knock on the door of every member of the *ton* demanding to know if they or their servants are the Brazen Belle?" Persephone looked entirely unbothered, even though there was no doubt who 'Lady P__ C__' was.

Her perfectly delectable mouth curved upward at the left corner. She found this amusing?

The scandal sheet crumbled in his hand. "Perhaps I will do precisely that, Persephone."

Her dark eyes flashed.

Maybe she wasn't as indifferent as she seemed. Edward should have taken it as a warning. Should have walked away that very moment, parting ways with her forevermore. She would never forgive him. Persephone would never be his.

Even if he would always be hers.

But that flash in her eyes lit something inside of him that he had not dared to acknowledge even existed—*hope*.

"And how many of the ladies who open their doors will invite you into their beds?" Persephone said sharply, rounding on him in the middle of the path.

It doesn't matter. None of them are you.

But he couldn't say it.

He couldn't deny her claim, either.

Instead, he kept his mouth shut, just barely. It was either that, or declare that he was still desperately in love with her... which seemed like it would not be well received.

Persephone's sharp little chin stabbed the air just as her finger flicked the edge of the scandal sheet. "Just as I thought. You've earned this reputation through your own misdeeds."

He had no defense for that. None that she'd want to hear.

"I am not the same man I was ten years ago," he finally said. It was a struggle to keep the emotion from his voice before the one person he'd never had to dissemble for.

Persephone arched one dark eyebrow, and Edward had to shove his hand into his pocket to still the impulse to reach up and smooth it over.

But she tracked the movement with her eyes. She knew how

much she was needling him. She might even be doing it purposefully. Though to what end, Edward wasn't sure. Which needled him—and inflamed him—even more. She'd always possessed an impressively devious mind. One thing that had not changed in the last ten years.

He still had not figured out why she'd sought him out at all. He would have seen the scandal sheet eventually without her shoving it under his nose.

Edward forced himself to take a long, controlled exhale before speaking again, trying to convince himself as much as her. "This is just another scandal sheet; another jilted lady trying to get in her jabs."

He saw instantaneously the effect the word had on her.

Ten years, almost to the day, since he'd done just that—jilted her. Left her behind with nothing but broken promises.

It had been the right decision then. *But now...*

"The Season has barely even begun," he said. The least he could do was try to assuage her unease over the scandal sheet. Maybe she'd hunted him down out of sheer anger. "There will be a new scandal next week, and this will be all but forgotten."

Her dark eyes narrowed and her petite nostrils flared as she leaned forward. She ran her finger underneath the lapel of his greatcoat, as if she could tell just how fine the wool was through her kidskin gloves. Edward barely managed to keep in the shuddering breath. She was so close to touching him. Even with layers of fabric between them, he imagined he'd be able to feel the heat of her skin.

Then flicked his shoulder, stepping back.

"How very male of you," she said. One of her dark curls came loose as she shook her head. "I'll not detain you any longer. I've done my good deed for the month."

Edward opened his mouth to try and generate an excuse to keep her at his side a few moments longer.

She walked to a waiting carriage he hadn't noticed before,

swaying her hips as she went. Her form-fitting pelisse tortured him with every step. His hand was already fisted in his pocket. Only once the door to the carriage closed and the team pulled away did the tension in his grasp finally ease.

But his knuckles didn't brush against carefully folded paper.

There was only silk.

That couldn't be—did he have a hole in his pocket?

He swung around, eyes examining the walkway, looking for any sign of the ransom note on the ground, even as realization crawled up his throat like bile.

She'd tapped that damned scandal sheet repeatedly. Caressing his lapel, flicking his shoulder. Distractions—so she could pilfer the ransom note from his pocket unnoticed.

That was what she'd been up to. The whole interaction had been a ruse to get the ransom note. No doubt, she intended to find Alfred on her own. It was so perfectly Persephone. She may never forgive him, but she'd always had a soft spot for Alfred. If she thought he was truly in danger, in need of her help, she would never let it alone.

That brilliant mind of hers was indeed every bit as sharp as it had been. Further honed by her work as the Lady Fixer. He could not help but be impressed.

"Bloody hell."

A storm of whispers erupted behind him. Three elderly dames, dressed in their muffs and woolens and looking utterly offended. One of them grasped a sheet that looked dangerously like the one currently disintegrating in Edward's fist.

Persephone no doubt hoped he would think he'd misplaced the note. That she'd never have to see him again. But that flicker in her gaze stayed with him, making a relentless demand.

Hope.

Maybe this was the perfect opportunity. Maybe his status in the world had changed enough. Maybe he could win her back.

He spun on his heel and stalked in the opposite direction, far away from the hotel, from the watchful eyes of polite society. He needed time to think, to plan.

He had misjudged everything.

Persephone did not need his protection.

He was the one who needed to be protected from her.

Chapter Five

Maybe it was a little bit cruel, stealing the ransom note that Edward needed in order to find his brother. But so long as the week ended with Alfred safe, did it really matter?

She dipped her quill pen in the inkpot again, scribbling out a few more lines of notes in her notebook. She had not decided if she would try and slip the ransom note back into his pocket at some future juncture, or whether she'd let Edward assume he'd lost it. In either case, she did not have much time to spare. The note was quite specific as to time and location.

Edward was rich enough to pay the ransom. But she would find Alfred before it came to that. And prove Edward wrong in the process. She may be called the Lady Fixer, but that did not mean she could not solve a man's problem. Honestly, most of the problems she solved for her clients were caused by men, one way or another.

The nib darted across the blank pages of her notebook, drawing arrows to connect ideas, scribbling out words and writing new ones. Her methodology appeared frantic at first glance, but it was the best way she'd ever devised for capturing the thoughts that danced around her mind.

She glanced up from her needlework to the clock on the mantle of the Marchioness of Clydon's exquisite sitting room. Right as the hour hand ticked upward to the three, the doors of the sitting room opened and Madison Warsham entered.

"Tea for two, then," Madison said over her shoulder to the butler as she seated herself on the chaise across where Persephone was stationed at the little rosewood writing desk. "Having a quiet afternoon?"

"Just writing down a few errant thoughts." Persephone snapped her notebook closed by habit.

But Madison was not even looking at her, too busy perusing a stack of newssheets delivered from across England. Persephone thought she spotted one all the way from Edinburgh. Persephone liked to stay apprised of current events, but Madison was nearing what Persephone would describe as an obsession.

"Anything of particular interest?" Persephone asked after the tea was poured. Her mother and father would expect a letter from her soon. So far, all she had to put in it were her tasks as the fixer —which she didn't intend to tell them about, her determination to uncover a kidnapping—unlikely to meet their approval, and a scandal sheet.

News, however placid, seemed the better alternative.

"Prinny would do well to make amends with the Princess of Wales. The quiet after Peterloo will not last," Madison said, tea in one hand as her eyes scanned the broadsheet in the other.

Persephone tried not to be too obvious about her confusion. She'd been woefully out of touch with the intricacies of London gossip while in New York. "What does one have to do with the other?"

Madison lifted her golden eyebrows over the top of the newssheet in her hand. This one was from Manchester. "Caroline of Brunswick is an intriguing political figure. She could turn public opinion in her favor."

Persephone nearly spilled her tea onto the desk. "As what?"

"A martyr."

Persephone did pause at that. "You think there will be another armed uprising?"

Her father was an astute parliamentarian. Surely he would not have gone abroad if he thought more unrest was possible.

Madison pursed her lips over her teacup. "I think Parliament and the Home Office would be naïve to imagine the threat is over."

Persephone shook her head over her needlework, which suddenly seemed so terribly insignificant. "You ought to be serving in the House of Lords."

Madison's smile curved wickedly. "Maybe someday women will have enough power to demand our due. For now, I will satisfy myself with sharing my every thought and theory with my husband."

"And he is amenable, the Marquess?" Persephone could just picture Henry Warsham patiently listening to his wife, while simultaneously distracting her with affectionate kisses.

That wicked smile stretched even further. "He's learned to be."

The pure satisfaction on Madison's face made Persephone's heart ache.

A love match, that was what the marquess and marchioness had. They understood each other on a deep level. Their wants and needs, their deepest desires. Madison was a woman with a mind sharp enough to slice. Her husband loved her enough to recognize and value it.

Did Persephone have any chance of finding such a match?

She'd told herself she would be content with affection, children, and the ability to continue her work helping the ladies of

London. But after a few months in the Warsham household, she wasn't sure it would be enough.

"Have any gentlemen caught your eye since your return to London?" Madison asked without even a hint of mock casualness.

A singularly familiar face appeared in her mind.

That was not an option.

"You are terribly obvious," Persephone said, trying to dislodge the vision.

Madison flashed a grin. "I rarely try to be anything but."

I am not the same man I was ten years ago, Edward had said.

In some ways, maybe it was true. Edward was no longer the mere son of a ship captain and a half-Chinese immigrant. His father had been wealthy before, but now Edward had his own fortune. He attended balls alongside the *ton*, something that had been unthinkable when they first met.

Our match would be an abomination. Your own relatives wouldn't receive you. I do not want that kind of life. He'd also said those things to her. The day after she'd been given the cut direct by the Countess of Tillbury while at court with her mother and father, because of her relationship with Edward. He should have consoled her. Promised her their love was strong enough to overcome an obstacle. Instead, he had broken her heart.

"There is no one," Persephone said. She set her tea on the table and opened her notebook once more, effectively ending the conversation.

But before Persephone could pick up her quill pen, the door to the sitting room opened and the Warsham's elderly butler appeared.

"Lady Persephone, there is a gentleman here to see you."

Madison's expression turned absolutely gleeful. "You spoke too soon, it seems."

Persephone tried to ignore the flicker of hope in her gut. Maybe her prospects were not as dismal as she'd feared. She had a gentleman caller. One could be parlayed into more, if she was clever. She shoved Edward from her mind. He had no right to be there, in any case. She would find his younger brother and then be free of him. Finally.

"Who is it?" Madison asked, newssheets discarded.

"Mr. Edward Johns, my lady."

Madison's eyes swung around too quickly for Persephone to hide her surprise.

"It is not what you think," Persephone said quickly, setting aside her notebook and quill pen. "Mr. Johns is an old acquaintance."

Madison's smile was nearly blinding. So she *had* seen *The Rake Review* that morning. "How interesting." But she clearly had not made the connection between Persephone's brooding and the gentleman waiting in the foyer.

Persephone tried not to melt under the pressure of that smile. Even as anger rose in her gut, her practical mind screamed at her. It may be beneficial to allow Madison to believe there was some sort of rapprochement between her and Edward. She was more likely to leave them alone. Which would give Persephone the opportunity to strangle him.

She averted her eyes as she spoke. "As I said, we were acquainted many years ago, before I left for New York."

From beneath her eyelashes, Persephone could see that Madison desperately wanted to press for more information. However, there was a gentleman waiting in the foyer.

"Admit him, of course," Madison said to the butler.

Persephone had just enough time to straighten her skirts and pat her curls before Edward strode through the doorway. He'd always walked with such purpose. It was one of the first things she had noticed about him all those years ago. Society may judge him as less, but he never allowed himself to be cowed by it. He stood taller, reasoned more clearly, earned his father's shipping company a fortune to rival any noble lord in England. And he looked damn handsome while doing it.

"Mr. Johns!" Madison exclaimed, offering her hand and executing a perfect curtsey.

"Lady Warsham, Lady Persephone." Edward bowed to them both, offering polite salutations to the lady of the house.

But his eyes were on Persephone.

The nearly black orbs burned.

Well, that answered one question. He'd figured out her little theft.

Madison, of course, continued on with what Persephone felt sure was mock obliviousness.

"It is a supreme pleasure to welcome you. I do not believe you have ever been a guest in my home," Madison said, clasping her hands together in poorly contained glee.

Edward dragged his gaze back to their host. "I am afraid not, my lady."

"Then this is quite the occasion," Madison said excitedly. Then she turned to the door and started walking. "If you will excuse me, I think I hear my daughter calling."

Edward's face screwed up in confusion as their hostess—their chaperone, the person making this audience acceptable and not a cause for ruination—walked out of the sitting room on a nonexistent pretext.

"*She* is supposed to be your chaperone?" he asked, incredulous. "She didn't even leave the door ajar."

Persephone bit her lower lip hard. How dare he come in and make aspersions against her hostess. How dare he look so damn handsome when he stared at her like he wanted to turn her upside down and shake her until the ransom note fell out of her pocket. She shoved both of those thoughts down.

"Lady Warsham is unconventional," she said. Her hands curved around the writing desk behind her, holding it tight to keep herself anchored in the sea of emotions swirling around her.

Edward advanced a step. "She is a walking scandal."

"And yet, her name did not appear in any scandal sheets this morning." Persephone lifted one hand to her hip.

Edward tracked the motion with his eyes. "Only because the *ton* is so used to her ridiculous antics that they cease to be newsworthy."

"And your exploits are newsworthy?" she asked sharply.

She did not want to talk about his exploits. The mere thought of him with another woman... she wanted to grab the crystal clock from the mantel and hurl it across the room. Heavens above. When had her temper become so intractable?

Edward watched her carefully, a mere yard of space separating them. He crossed his arms over his chest before he spoke.

"You refuse to help me find Alfred, then you steal the ransom note. What are you up to, Persephone?" he asked. Nay, demanded.

As if he had any right to demand *anything* from her.

She should have insisted he call her Lady Persephone. But hearing her name on his lips... she just could not bring herself to correct him.

Would he taste the same as he had all those years ago? A mix of briny salt and coffee that she still dreamed about. He licked his lower lip slowly. Not intentionally, she told herself. He was not intentionally trying to entice her. But it was effective nonetheless.

She could not fall back into love with Edward Johns.

"Congratulations on locating my residence. You were quicker than I anticipated," she snapped.

Edward did not respond to her barb. He merely considered her with that patient, even look upon his face.

Arse.

She smiled, even though it felt wrong. "Not what a gentleman wants to hear?"

But once again, Edward ignored her jab. There was a slight tick at the corner of his left eye, but she was not sure what it meant. He hadn't possessed that particular tell when she'd known him before.

"You are trying to incite a quarrel. If you truly refuse to help me, if you truly do not care for Alfred's fate, then return the note." Edward held out his hand expectantly.

"I am going to find Alfred. Not because it is what you want, but because it is the decent thing to do," Persephone snapped. She hated how childish it sounded. That was not her. She was kind, open-hearted. She'd made helping people her life's work.

Edward's face softened instantly. He took another step toward her, his long stride bringing him dangerously close. There was the damn scent of his bergamot and anise soap again.

"What have you been able to discern from the note?" Edward asked, peering over her shoulder toward the writing desk.

Persephone stiffened. "No. I will find Alfred. On my own. Without you."

Edward rocked back on his heels as if she'd physically struck him. His brow creased, his voice gravelly as he said, "Absolutely not."

"You need me," she insisted.

The dark look that crossed his face nearly stole her breath. It couldn't be... no. She could not allow that thought to even enter her mind. She muscled past it.

"I suppose you already know that this note," she paused to tug the ransom note out of her décolletage, "was written by a woman. And a well-educated one at that, given the spelling and penmanship."

Edward's eyes darted downward. To the note, not to the slice of cleavage visible just above the square neckline of her blue gown, she assured herself.

"No? Well then, surely you're aware that the writer was left handed?" That had been the first thing she noticed—the slight slant of the letters.

He hadn't realized either, she could see from his frown. He was staring at the letter as if it might come to life and bite him.

How would he respond if *she* bit him?

The horror of that thought sent her mind careening. How had she gone from refusing to help Edward, to determining she'd find Alfred on her own, to convincing Edward he needed her help? Was she the one being manipulated?

She thrust the note at him. If her hands were shaking slightly... well, she ignored that.

"I rescind my offer. Hire a private investigator. I have no time for this," she said.

"I am in London to find a husband," she said quietly, under her breath.

But not quietly enough.

Edward made a terrible sound. Half-strangled, gravelly and hard.

"A husband?"

Maybe it was the rawness of his tone. Or maybe it was the fact that her supposedly brilliant mind seemed to malfunction when in Edward's presence. *Something* must account for the fact that she answered him at all.

"I desire a family, and for that I need a husband. I have had disappointingly few prospects since returning to London, despite my position and my dowry. That is where I need to dedicate my attention." She should not take on any more clients, other than the two she'd already committed to, and she certainly should not be investigating a kidnapping well outside the scope of any of her previous work. If she wanted anything even close to the reality that Madison, Henry, and Nora had shown her, she needed to focus her attention.

Her cheeks burned with embarrassment. She should not have said any of it in front of Edward, of all people. But she forced herself to be brave, to look up and meet his gaze.

For a heartbeat, Edward's face was totally unmoved. He stared at her like she'd taken leave of her senses. No, like he hadn't heard her at all. Then for the briefest second, a maelstrom of emotions flashed across his handsome visage.

The force of them, even for the mere second he allowed them to be there, set Persephone's mind tumbling.

That couldn't have been pain in his face. That wasn't possible. Not after all this time.

But when she blinked, Edward's expression was calm and resolute.

"Use my scandalous reputation to your advantage," he said.

Persephone blinked. Once, twice. Certain she had misheard them. Once again grabbing the rosewood writing desk to keep herself upright. She must have been shaking her head in disbelief, because Edward continued.

"Men want what other men have. If we pretend to have an understating, to be courting, other gentlemen will take notice. My reputation is not what it once was; being seen with me will not be damaging to you now. After the Brazen Belle's article, it can only help you attract notice."

The words were sharp and painful, even if he had not meant them to be.

Edward stepped closer, into her space. "I help you gain suitors so you can find yourself a husband. You help me find Alfred."

It might work.

But oh, how cruel it would be.

How cruel that the man who had jilted her because of what his presence in her life would mean to her status was now in a position to use his status to help her gain what she wanted.

"How ironic it is," she said quietly. "You jilted me because of the damage you imagined our relationship would do to my own status and reputation. Now, you propose to use your elevated position to help me raise mine."

That corner of his eye was twitching again. More insistently.

Until Edward had to lift a hand to it, pressing his palm to the corner of his eye.

Realization hit her.

He *was* hurting.

Maybe not the way she was, where her heart threatened to burst in her chest just at the prospect of intentionally spending time with him. But he hadn't walked away from their failed engagement unscathed either.

Good.

She'd spent the months after he left her, first in London and then in New York, hoping he was hurting even half as badly as she. He deserved it.

But it didn't bring the satisfaction she'd always expected.

Persephone felt herself deflating, even as she knew she should be standing strong and refusing his ridiculous proposal.

She wished it didn't bother her as much as it did. She wished she had stayed in New York. She wished... well, she needed to stop wishing. Wishing for the impossible had only earned her a broken heart where Edward Johns was concerned.

At least if he was working with her, he would be too busy to bed everything female that moved in London. Persephone should not have cared.

"Once we have found Alfred, and restored my status among the *ton*, you will let me alone," she said. If that was pain flashing in Edward's eyes... well, she had her own pain to attend to. She could not be responsible for his. The pain had been his doing from the start.

"As you wish," Edward said, inclining his head.

He was still much, much too close to her. Close enough that the scent of him was making her light-headed. She could not decide if she wanted to throttle him or kiss him.

Persephone's traitorous heart wished for the latter.

Chapter Six

In his thirty years of life, Edward had never attended a charity event. He oversaw his family's contribution to many charitable endeavors—primarily those which benefited immigrants or orphans. His mother's preference, not his.

But the only reason that Edward himself interacted with the *ton* was out of necessity, be it physical or financial. To fill the hole in his chest or to fill his family's accounts.

Charity events did not scream of seduction.

Yet there he stood, with Persephone on one arm and the Marchioness of Clydon near the other, as a swirl of primarily female patrons made idle talk around him. Persephone insisted this event would both help them identify the woman who had written the ransom note, and function as one of the three society events she'd agreed to attend with him. *Limiting the amount of time we must spend in one another's company*, she'd said so sharply it had nearly cut him.

He would attend a hundred charity events if that is what it took to win back Persephone's heart.

Walking alone in the brisk January air, all the way from the

Pendleton in Mayfair to his family home in Limehouse, Edward had realized three things.

The first—he was completely, utterly, and irrevocably in love with Persephone Cuthbert. Ten years and an ocean had not been enough to erase what he felt for her. He doubted a lifetime would be sufficient. And from the glint in her eyes, the emotions boiling so near the surface first at the ball and then in the park... maybe, just maybe, Persephone was still in love with him as well, even though she believed that love impossible. Which had brought him to his second realization.

He was not the same man he'd been a decade ago. He was wealthy, begrudgingly accepted by the ton. Marriage to him would not be the challenge he'd tried to save her from all those years ago.

The third realization was that perhaps he had been wrong in the first place. That realization was the one he chose not to examine too closely.

But if he still loved Persephone, and she still loved him, and society would allow them a chance at happiness, then Edward would take that chance.

He was not a gambling man. He prided himself on carefully thought out decisions. Perfect decorum was how he survived in the *ton*. But he would do just about anything to earn back Persephone's love.

It started with securing her help in finding Alfred. A week until the deadline in the ransom note. A week in which they would be forced to spend time together, investigating. Like this evening, at the charity auction.

Not his ideal choice for a seduction. But convincing Persephone that he was a different man—a man worth loving again— was going to take more than seduction. He would need every opportunity.

Offering himself as the conduit to achieving the esteem of the gentlemen of the *ton* had not been part of his plan when he arrived at the Marquess and Marchioness of Clydon's mansion.

The mere notion of Persephone in another man's arms, another man's wife, was enough to make him ill. There was one way this week, this agreement between them, was going to end.

With Persephone in *his* arms. Forever.

The scent of vanilla and cinnamon accosted his senses a second before a voice whispered in his ear.

"I know you are better at pretending than this," Persephone said, pitching her tone low enough that only he would hear. On his other side, the marchioness was smiling and talking with their host for the evening, Lady Wheeler.

Edward had not even realized he was frowning. Determination, not distaste. Though he supposed to everyone else, they looked the same. He forced himself to soften his brow and unclench his jaw.

He led Persephone deeper into the townhouse, where the busy foyer opened into a drawing room. Now that there were dozens of eyes to watch them, keeping close to their chaperone's side was not strictly necessary.

Persephone spared him another taunt until they were in the drawing room hovering near a punch bowl.

"I cannot be so repulsive that you can't manage even a smile or pseudo-romantic glance," she said. Edward wasn't certain that he imagined the slight hurt tinging her voice.

"Charity auctions are not romantic," he said, his voice low. Light. Teasing.

Persephone looked at him as if he had grown a second head.

There were not enough guests to slip out unnoticed, nor was there a network of rooms open where a romantically inclined couple might retreat for a tryst. No balcony or garden for a rendezvous—not that Edward had much desire for one in the frigid January air.

If he was searching for a new conquest, this was not the place for it.

Though perhaps that was why Persephone had selected it for the first of their three agreed upon outings. Only a serious suitor would escort a lady to such an event.

"Is there much romance involved in your interactions with the ladies of the *ton*?" she asked, gripping his arm tighter.

He managed not to flinch at the accusation underlying her words.

She did not truly want to know the answer to that question, and they both knew it.

But Edward couldn't resist. He wanted to push her further. He leaned forward into her space, until his mouth was just above her ear and her mouth was less than an inch from the sharp line of his jaw. He could feel the warmth of her breath. He knew she could feel his by the delightfully torturous way she shivered against him.

"What do you think?" he murmured into the shell of her ear.

The angle was just a bit too sharp for him to discern if a blush climbed up her perfectly curved throat to color her cheeks.

"I think you are every bit the rake I have been warned about," she bit out. But she did not step away.

Because this was exactly what she wanted? Or because she felt that inexorable pull just as strongly as he did?

Their plan only succeeded if the other members of society noticed the special attention he paid her. There may be a shortage of eligible gentlemen in attendance tonight. But their sisters and mothers were there, ready to carry back word of the special attention Mr. Edward Johns paid to Lady Persephone Cuthbert, to wonder at just what about the duke's daughter had caught the rake's notoriously roving eye.

"You sound disappointed." He was the rake she believed him to be. *But that stops here, now.* Truly, it had stopped when he saw her across the ballroom clad in sapphire with a white rose in her hair.

Persephone lifted her chin, pale skin glowing like ivory in the evening light. "The man I used to love didn't need to find validation between a woman's thighs."

How wrong she was. He'd always wanted approval—but only from one woman. Everyone else was merely a distraction. A piss poor attempt to fill the gaping void inside of him once Persephone was no longer in his life.

He wanted to push her against the wall and claim her lips. To show her that the only woman he'd ever wanted was the one currently on his arm. That the love she referenced so casually burned inside of him still. To tell her that love was the reason he'd let her go in the first place.

But she was not ready for that. Not yet.

* * *

Watching Persephone was only minimally better than touching her.

She worked her way through the litany of guests with an ease that spoke to her years in New York. She hadn't spent them holed up, moping and mourning their broken engagement. As she spoke with the other ladies in attendance, she smiled easily, laughed often, and left those in her wake with their own smiles and laughter to match.

Once, he'd been the recipient of those smiles.

The memory was as clear to him now as it had been ten years ago. The soft candlelight of the drawing room in Portsmouth, decorated in reds and golds to match the fall foliage outside the windows. The din of voices, mostly female. So many of the gentlemen away on the Continent, rallying against Napoleon.

Persephone's father, the duke, was in Portsmouth before deploying to Spain. Persephone had not even had her first season.

The small party was an indulgence by her parents for a beloved youngest daughter.

So many tiny occurrences could have prevented their meeting.

If Edward had eaten at home earlier in the week, instead of breaking his fast in a dockside pub and meeting the son of the Earl of Cavendish. A coincidence which led to his invitation to the soiree.

If she had chosen to remain in London with her elder brother and his wife, rather than venture to Portsmouth with her mother to see her father for a few brief days.

If he'd gotten held up at the shipping office.

If she hadn't been able to borrow an evening gown from an acquaintance.

But he had. And she had.

And the moment that Persephone Cuthbert had caught his eye across the crowded sitting room and smiled at him, Edward had been lost.

Those smiles were not directed at him anymore, and he'd more than earned it. He had done everything in his power to make sure that Persephone would never smile at him again.

Maybe he was a fool for hoping. The flash in her eyes could have been ire as easily as repressed desire or affection. But he would use this week to do everything within his power to convince her that he was a different man. A worthy man.

He'd saved Alfred from a dozen scrapes such as this one over the past several years. The wastrel would have to languish a few days longer in whatever pleasure den he'd constructed for himself. If he was a little uncomfortable while he waited to be found, it was no less than he deserved. So long as their parents were spared from dealing with Alfred's nonsense, Edward felt no guilt for using the situation to his advantage.

Not even where Persephone was concerned.

At least he did not have to fake the longing in his gaze as he watched her across the crowded sitting room.

He set down the punch glass—when had he even emptied it? —before it could shatter under the pressure of his grip.

There had to be something stronger on offer. This charity auction may be primarily attended by women, but there was at least one gentleman resident in the house. Which meant there had to be a decanter somewhere.

"Good evening, Mr. Johns," said a sultry voice that sounded of smoke and nighttime.

The contrast to the bright tone he'd been hearing in his mind was jarring. But Edward did not allow that to play across his face. He did not allow any emotion at all, snapping his usual taciturn mask into place.

"Madam," he nodded by habit, effecting a half bow that had served him well when he did not know the exact status of the person he addressed. All of them were higher ranked than the half-Chinese son of a merchant.

She did not offer any further information, merely dragged her gaze up and down his frame with a sense of proprietorship that immediately set him on edge.

"I do not believe we are acquainted," he said, already lifting his gaze over her shoulder to locate Persephone.

"I am a dear friend of Viscountess Bampton," the woman purred.

That snagged his attention. Edward looked at the woman— truly looked at her. The gown was a bit too daring for a charity function, the thrust of her breasts just shy of indecent. But it was the tilt of her mouth that gave her away.

A mouth curved in silent demand. Want. Entitlement.

A dear friend of Viscountess Bampton.

It was the easiest way to drive him away. A rake he might be, but he chose his conquests—not the other way around.

Play nice, a voice that sounded suspiciously like his mother's admonished in his head.

He was supposed to be courting Persephone. He *was* courting Persephone. But Persephone did not realize it.

Edward resisted the urge to massage his temples. Complicated interactions and nuances had always been Persephone's strength, not his.

A serious suitor would not make a scene at an event where he'd escorted his lady love. He'd be perfectly polite. Which should have been easy, since Edward always played by the rules. He couldn't afford to jeopardize the tenuous bonds he'd formed on behalf of the company his father had built, Johns Maritime Enterprises. But tonight, there was even more at stake.

Carefully, he angled his body away so that there was a wide triangle of space between them, opening out to the rest of the drawing room. Guests were beginning to seat themselves in the rows of chairs. The auction would begin soon, thanks be to God.

"Unfortunately, I am not available this evening," Edward said.

Without meaning to, his eyes drifted to Persephone.

The lady, whose name he had not even been given before she'd propositioned him, followed his gaze.

"Miss Cuthbert?" she said archly.

Edward's gut twisted. "Lady Persephone," he corrected, trying and failing to moderate the clip of his words.

"Lady Persephone..." the woman said, brows lifting. She was also adept at hiding her emotions. But Edward had spent a lifetime learning to judge others, to anticipate their reactions. For him, it had been a skill born of self-preservation. He easily read the disdain around her words as she added, "Yes, I see."

He was done with this conversation. If it continued, he'd embarrass himself and Persephone both by tossing this woman aside, bodily. But before his foot hit the floor, the lady moved. Quickly, trapping him in the corner.

She crooked her finger under the lapel of his tailcoat. "There is a butler's pantry near the staircase that is not in use this evening."

This time, Edward did not cloak the emotion that rose to his face. He let the revulsion play across his features for the lady to see. She rocked back as if struck, yanking her hand away.

Only to be met with Persephone's blinding smile.

"Lady Manrow, have times really changed so much?"

Chapter Seven

The charity event was dual purpose. Or perhaps tri-purpose?

"Oh, yes, Miss Anna Winlock has a reticule just like it that I have always admired," said young Miss Goodwin after Persephone made a point of flashing her own ornate reticule. Miss Goodwin did not recall when she'd last seen Miss Anna's missing accessory, but she confirmed that it was oft-admired by other ladies of the *ton*.

"My Sarah received several calls from the younger Mr. St. James last season, but then his attention seemed to ebb. It was all quite strange," the Countess of Mansfield reported. A few more questions, and Persephone was able to deduce within a week when Lady Olivia St. James' son had begun the affair his mother was so concerned about.

Very satisfactory progress on the two tasks she'd accepted at the first ball of the season. She allowed herself a celebratory comfit as two longtime friends of her mother, Lady Carr and Lady Bartleby, chatted amiably.

"How lovely that you've brought along Mr. Johns. I shared more than one dance with his father during my debut season,"

Lady Carr blissfully recalled. Having met Edward's father, Persephone understood the wistful remembrance. Edward had inherited his broad shoulders and handsome face from his father.

But more importantly, the sentiment was positive. Which meant that despite—or maybe because of—the Rake Review column, Edward was indeed suddenly considered a desirable prospect. One who'd arrived on her arm.

She hated that he was right.

Even more than that, she hated that the very reason he'd given all those years ago for jilting her was now irrelevant.

Not that it changed anything between them. Whatever feeling she still held for Edward was dwarfed in comparison to the anger she felt, Persephone reminded herself.

She finished her comfit, made her excuses, and drifted off to the next group of women. As she worked her way around the drawing room, she kept her ears alert for any bit of information that might advance her progress in finding the missing reticule or hinted at young Mr. St. James' mistress. But when she spoke, her focus was on Alfred. Or rather, casually dropping in comments that would help her find the left-handed young woman who had written the ransom note.

"Your niece is left handed? What a shame. I believe Mrs. Haverford's youngest was as well, and they engaged a tutor to break her of it. I shall see if I can obtain the name for you," Mrs. Hayes offered kindly in response to Persephone's artfully casual comment.

Persephone thanked her profusely, asking her to send word to the Warsham residence. If the charity auction was not as productive as she hoped, the tutor would be a good source for finding left-handed ladies who might have written the ransom note.

Quad-purpose. Not a real word, but accurate to the situation.

Persephone rewarded herself with a canape drizzled in honey. She had such a weakness for honey. In her tea, on her toast, drizzled over pastries—

Why was Edward in the corner?

She'd been tracking him casually all evening, making certain that the women she spoke with noted her wistful glances in his direction. But she'd been sidetracked by the honey-soaked bite of deliciousness.

In those few lost moments, Edward had gained a companion.

The honey turned bitter in Persephone's mouth. She recognized the svelte figure even from across the sitting room.

Suddenly, she was right behind them—behind *her*.

How had she gotten there? She did not even recall walking.

Persephone worked out possibilities, she examined angles of attack and reviewed outcomes. In her head, on paper. She thought about everything.

But there was no thinking then.

Not when the older woman slid her hand beneath the lapel of Edward's tailcoat and *purred*.

"Lady Manrow, have times really changed so much?" Persephone barely dodged the woman as she staggered backward. Too fast—not from her words, but from something Edward had said or done.

But the lady's eyes were on Persephone now, narrowing with an emotion that she did not bother to cloak.

Loathing.

"I am afraid I do not take your meaning, Lady Persephone," she said, landing her palm just above her breast and slowly sweeping it down along the curve of her body.

The dress she wore, while technically the column style so popular in London, was too small. Persephone had no doubt it was an intentional choice, meant to show off her perfectly proportioned curves.

Persephone did not allow her blinding smile to falter even a fraction of an inch.

"I do apologize, I should speak more slowly when addressing a lady of your esteemed age," she said brightly. As she spoke, she maneuvered her much larger, much curvier body into the space left by Lady Manrow's backward step.

She placed one hand on Edward's arm and the other on the broad lapel of his tailcoat. Precisely where Lady Manrow's fingers had been moments before. Except that Edward did not push her away. His face was unreadable, but that was the expression he wore most of the time anyway.

Persephone did not even glance back at Lady Manrow as she spoke in the same tone she used when explaining something to a child— "It is only that my governess was quite explicit in her instruction that it is rude to try to take something that belongs to someone else."

Lady Manrow blinked.

Persephone let out a little lovesick sigh as she slowly turned her gaze back to the older woman. "But rules of propriety do change over the decades. Why, it was a different century when you were in the schoolroom. Perhaps the instruction you received was substantively different."

Persephone hardly believed she was saying such a thing. She'd never insulted someone so brazenly in her entire life. Except Edward, in the last few days. But she certainly did not believe in anything so trite as demeaning someone for their age. Yet the words had come so easily.

The lady's eyes bulged in a most unattractive way, completely at odds with the seductive smirk she'd worn moments before. Persephone's heart was pounding hard enough, she was certain that if she looked down she'd see the vibration in her chest.

But she could not stop. She couldn't linger. She had to get Edward away. It was a visceral need to get him as far as possible from the woman who'd looked all but ready to climb him mere seconds ago.

She leaned up so that her mouth was near his jaw and said in a not-so-hushed whisper, "Come, my love."

Edward, for once, did not argue with her.

He didn't flinch as she slid down his body, nor as she gripped his hand and led him to the other side of the room, to the furthest chairs on the opposite aisle and far, far away from the fiery eyes of Lady Manrow.

He gave her all of three breaths before he spoke, his beautiful jaw working around the words. "If you wished to make a scene, you've certainly succeeded."

"I did not wish for any of this," she said sharply.

Her wishes were simple. Continue with the work that had given her life purpose in the months and years after Edward had left her, and find a husband so she could have a family with some semblance of the warmth she'd witnessed in the Warsham home.

Neither of those aims should have involved Edward. Yet she could only deal with events as she'd been presented with them. She *would* have her heart's desire. And this time, it would not include him.

She lifted the folded program that had been on her chair before she sat and began to examine it as she said idly, "If you could manage to stay out of trouble, none of that would have been necessary."

Edward made no move to look at the program in his own hand.

"I would not characterize Lady Manrow as trouble," he said.

Persephone did not allow herself to flinch. Of course, he wouldn't view the woman's wanton proposition as an imposition. He was a rake, and he'd earned the title by bedding women just like Lady Manrow.

But if he did not realize that even a conversation with the lady was dangerous to their bargain and their pursuit of Alfred... "Then you are as naïve as you are rakish. You are meant to be courting me. That was our agreement. My entire plan for this evening depends upon you being besotted with me. You are endangering both of our aims with your reck-lessness."

She felt him shift in the seat beside her, but did not allow herself to look up.

"I was not going to accept her offer," he said.

"So, she did make you an offer," she said, snapping the thick paper in the air. She wasn't able to feign nonchalance any longer. When she looked his way, Edward's near-black gaze was waiting.

"You knew that. Otherwise, you would not have been so jealous," he said.

"I am—I was not jealous," Persephone corrected herself. "I am merely preserving the integrity of our agreement. If anyone suspects that you are anything less than besotted with me, then my plan will not work."

He did not ask about her plan, which was damned odd. Did he truly care so little for his brother? What reason would he have to blindly trust her without demanding details?

Perhaps he had heard more about the Lady Fixer than she'd realized. It could be that he was finally giving her skills the respect they deserved. But that explanation did not sit quite right in her stomach.

"You are the one who appears to be besotted with me."

He was not wrong. That was exactly how she looked, dashing across the room and dragging him away. Which made her want to hit him in the bollocks, exactly as her elder brother had taught her before her first season.

"That only proves that I am holding up my end of the bargain better than you." She wanted to tear her eyes away, but there was a slight crinkle at the corner of Edward's eyes that sounded alarm bells in her mind.

That gaze... she did not want to hear what he would say next.

She should never have agreed to his proposal to fake a courtship. Seeking out Alfred on her own would have been infinitely safer. The more time she spent with him, the more she remembered what had attracted her to him at first. And the more danger she was in of making a very foolish mistake.

She snapped her head forward to where their hosts of the evening, Lord and Lady Wheeler, had come to stand on the makeshift stage.

"The auction is starting. Do your best to spend it looking at me with adoration and unfulfilled longing," she said without a sideways glance.

Edward was thankfully silent as Lady Wheeler cleared her throat and called the event to order. She began by thanking the guests in advance for their generosity to benefit the Charity League for Orphans, then thanking the patrons who'd donated the items they would be bidding upon tonight. A servant passed out paddles. Persephone took one even though she had no intention of bidding. Edward did as well.

On the other side of the room, Madison waved and accepted a paddle, her own husband having begged off attending the event. Of course, Madison should have been at Persephone's side, chaperoning. So, naturally, the woman was on the complete opposite side of the room.

A terrible, but quite useful, chaperone.

"Bid when I tell you," Persephone murmured to Edward. Again, keeping her gaze very purposefully forward. If she did not look at him, she could fend off the wave of emotions he inspired.

"What are you planning in that brilliant mind of yours?"

Persephone's heart did a dangerous little jig inside her chest. Her fingers curled tighter around the paddle in her lap.

"All of the guests have seen us here together. They will be watching us. If you bid on an expensive item, it will draw interest to me, and hopefully earn an invitation from Lady Wheeler," she explained.

"What does any of that have to do with Alfred?" Edward asked, scooting closer to her. Close enough that his knee brushed against hers. He may as well have lit a firecracker inside of her.

But Lord Wheeler began the bidding, and there was no time for a response. He would just have to trust her.

The first item came up for bid, then the second. Persephone did not glance Edward's way once, not even to verify if he was doing his part with those adoring stares. She had to trust that he loved his brother enough to do as she said.

That thought steadied her. Edward loved his family fiercely. It was one of the things she'd most admired about him. While a lesser man might have tried to distance himself, to pass for wholly English and avoid the abuse he'd endured since childhood, Edward was ferociously protective of his mother and younger brother. His father, of course, the grandson of a duke, could fend for himself.

Which also eased her worries from earlier in the evening. He must be relying on accounts of her prowess as the Lady Fixer. It was the only reasonable explanation for his trust in her.

The third item passed, then the fourth. Madison bid on a week-long excursion to the Duke of Abercorn's country estate in Ireland. In any other circumstance, it would have been gauche to even consider exchanging money for the purpose of visiting another peer's estate. But this was for charity. Nearly anything could be excused.

Which was precisely what Persephone was depending upon.

The second to last item came up for bid, and Persephone tilted her head to the left. "Now."

Edward did not move. She nudged him in the ribs.

Still, the paddle didn't lift, even as several others expressed their interest.

This was the second to last item. The most coveted item. She'd had to promise Lady Wheeler's daughter an introduction to her cousin in order to get a preview of the items available just so Edward could bid in this moment.

"You must bid," she whispered urgently.

Edward blinked at her, the confusion evident in his face "I do not want a matched pair of Arabians."

He detested riding. How had she forgotten that? She should

have picked a different item for him to bid on. But this was the most expensive, the one guaranteed to make the biggest statement and to get the biggest reaction.

"Tonight, you do," she whispered urgently.

Conflict washed over his face. "No, I do not."

"This is for Alfred!" she squeaked, though she had no time to explain. "Put your hand in the air or I will—"

Thank the heavens, he lifted it.

A near thing, as she hadn't had an action to finish her rash statement.

Only once Edward had lifted the paddle to bid twice more did she reorient herself toward to the front of the room, and her ears actually processed the sums that Lord Wheeler was calling out.

The price was going up quickly.

This was not what she'd intended.

That was the son of the Earl of Chambray, sitting beside his sister but sending not-so-subtle glances her way.

Then Viscount Hopp joined the fray, smiling at her with unabridged interest.

No. No, no, no, no, no.

She had not anticipated that Edward's plan would work this quickly. She'd only spent a few minutes in Edward's presence, yet that was apparently all it had taken to garner the interest of two men in attendance. One aim was not meant to interfere with the other. She needed Edward to win the pair of Arabians in order for the next piece of her plan to find Alfred to fall into place.

"They are bidding for you." Edward's words slid over her shoulders, along her neck until she was shivering.

"I know," she hissed. She had to brazen past the untenable desire that lifted in her at the bite of his words. Desire for Edward, when she was meant to be using him to find a husband. Heaven help her.

The bids continued, higher, higher, higher.

Each time, Edward raised his hand again.

It was impossible. He could not afford—

"The pair of Arabians, to Mr. Edward Johns for the sum of..." Lord Wheeler called out, but Persphone's mind was already on to the next part of her plan.

The crowd broke into more excited than polite applause at the sum expended—all in the interests of charity, of course. Not because of the entertainment of watching three men bid upon a previously unnoticed woman's attention.

Persephone would worry about that later.

Just then, she was busy contemplating a whole new line of actions and consequences and redirections.

"Lord Wheeler is a kind man. He will try to be discreet about passing the pair along to Viscount Hopp when you tell him you are unable to pay the final bid," she whispered to Edward, even as the attention shifted away from them and the final round of bidding began.

She knew that Edward was wealthy now, had verified it herself with a few carefully placed questions to Madison Warsham, her husband Henry, and a handful of their friends. But the amount of money that had been bid was enough that she knew even her father would have paused.

His dark eyes were fixed forward, but the corner of his mouth twitched.

"I can pay," he said.

Persephone cringed. She could not see the other side of his face to determine if his eye was twitching as well. But he was clearly repressing some emotion, and she doubted it was a favorable one.

"Edward, I... I should have spoken with you before. We could have bid on a less expensive item—"

"Persephone, I can pay for the pair of damned horses."

She worried her bottom lip to the point of painfulness, but it barely registered. "What will you father say?"

His chest lifted and fell in a silent chuckle. "He'll say I am a fool for wasting my hard-earned money on a pair of horses when I cannot stand the creatures, but other than that I imagine he and my mother will merely laugh at my expense over a glass of sherry."

"But the company…"

His eyes flashed with understanding, the corners of his mouth lifting into a smirk. "I will pay for the horses myself. My own funds are more than adequate."

My own funds are more than adequate.

What had he been doing for the last ten years?

Apparently, she'd asked the question aloud.

"I saved up my salary to buy several ships of my own. I crewed them for a few years, made a tidy profit, and then sold them to my father in exchange for a one third interest in the company."

While she'd been in New York, seeding herself with the upper crust of society so she could find missing reticules and catch wayward sons determined to sow their wild oats, Edward had built an entire shipping enterprise, then parlayed it into a substantial in his father's even bigger, even more profitable shipping company.

"You can pay for the horses yourself," she said softly.

"Quite easily," he confirmed.

Persephone's mind was doing uncomfortable twirls inside her head. She had never thought to look into the state of Johns Maritime Enterprises now, all these years later. She'd known Edward was ambitious. Of course, he'd been that way at twenty-one. But she'd expected that would manifest in a high-ranking position within the company, not owning part of it himself.

It was… an unfathomable accomplishment. Thirty-one years old and rich enough to rival any duke in England.

Edward's fingers brushed over her gloved hand. "I never thought I'd see it."

She stared at the sharp contrast of his skin against her midnight blue gloves before looking up at him in confusion. "What?"

"The day that Persephone Cuthbert was struck speechless."

She opened her mouth to say something—anything—but nothing came out.

Then, just as she was about to manage a retort, Edward was drawing her up to stand and tucking her gloved hand into his arm.

"Mr. Johns," Lady Wheeler exclaimed, her smile so wide it nearly touched her ears. "We are so very grateful for your contribution! The Charity League for Orphans will no doubt be overwhelmed by your goodwill!"

"It is my pleasure," he said politely.

Lady Wheeler waited a beat, as if she expected more of a response to her effusive thanks. Apparently, she was not very well acquainted with Edward. She turned to Persephone instead.

"Lady Persephone, I would be most honored if you would join us tomorrow afternoon. Several ladies in attendance tonight will be coming together to write thank-you notes to all of those who donated tonight. I am pleased to say that in addition to the larger items from the auction, we've received over a thousand pounds in smaller contributions as well. It will be quite a task, but we'd be honored to have your assistance."

"And I would be most honored to render it. Thank you for the invitation, Lady Wheeler. I accept gladly." Persephone reached across the space between them, careful to keep her other hand nestled affectionately in the crook of Edward's arm, and clasped the other woman's hand.

Lady Wheeler returned her squeeze, then moved off to thank the other guests who had made donations by bidding on items during the auction.

Persephone could feel the weight of Edward's gaze upon her, but she waited until they were well away from any other guests before she returned it.

"Thank you notes?" he asked from beneath an arched brow that accentuated the unfairly graceful arc of his eyes.

"It is not about writing the notes. It is about exclusivity. One must be able to expend an impressive amount of money in order to even garner an invitation. Every lady of note and her daughter, sister, or mother will be in attendance writing those thank you notes," she explained, letting her mouth curve upward in a triumphant smile. "More than a few of them are likely left-handed."

Edward's other brow rose to meet the first. But for several beats of her traitorous heart, he said nothing.

"I never thought I'd see it." Persephone grinned, not bothering to wait for a response. "The day that Edward Johns was struck speechless."

Chapter Eight

Walking away from Persephone was getting harder by the day.

Leaving her on the doorstep of the Marquess and Marchioness of Clydon's home had felt... wrong.

The only time Edward had ever felt truly right was when she was in his arms.

The hardest part of the evening had been not dragging her into the butler pantry that Lady Manrow had mentioned and showing her just what that little show of jealousy had done to him.

She would not feel jealous if she did not care.

He could have done without two horses he'd never used, however. Not the sort of careful expenditures that had made him wealthy. The Brazen Belle's mention of him raining trinkets upon his lovers was entirely fictitious. But when it came to Persephone, Edward could finally understand the temptation.

Watching her at the charity auction, it had been all too easy to forget the reason for their charade. Her charade. His feelings were entirely sincere.

Alfred was still missing. And Edward still had no intention of paying the ransom, which meant they had to find him soon. Persephone would chase down her plan, and Edward would do his part to investigate the few avenues he hadn't yet explored.

He ought to have resented the fact that he was not in his bed after a long, draining day. But protecting his younger brother was like breathing. He hardly thought about it; he'd been doing it for more than twenty years.

There was no punch leveled at Alfred that hadn't been answered with Edward's fists.

He would happily resort to fisticuffs if that could save Alfred from whatever trouble he'd stumbled into. Laughing, easy-going Alfred, who would rather drink rum with the sailors on their ships rather than ensure a shipment was properly loaded. He was well liked by everyone employed at the company, but he had not made any moves towards claiming the one third of shares that Edward knew his father was prepared to sell to him.

Not my business, Edward reminded himself. Relations had been tense between Alfred and their father for months. But it was not Edward's place to intervene. He'd protect Alfred as well as he could, insomuch as he could, from his own stupidity.

Which included saving him from whatever supposed villain had kidnapped him and left the ransom note—without telling their father that anything was amiss.

He waved away the offer from the Clydon's coachman to return him to the Pendleton. It was brutally cold, a thin layer of ice beginning to form over the muddy puddles in the road left from an afternoon of dismal rain. But Edward buttoned his greatcoat, pulled his topper down further over his ears, and kept walking.

Mayfair watched him as he walked, block by block.

Hyde Park.

Grosvenor Square.

White's.

Once, when he'd first come to London, he'd considered

seeking membership. But just as quickly as the thought had entered his young head, he'd dismissed it.

He'd been the son of a wealthy merchant, but with no real money or connections of his own. Even now, he did not allow himself to entertain the notion. Men like him, genteelly mannered and wealthy as he might be, did not become members of White's. Nor any of the other esteemed social clubs lining the streets of Mayfair.

But with enough walking, he reached a place where they always took his money.

La Rose Rouge.

If he never applied to White's, he would never be rejected.

It was a philosophy that had served him well in nearly every aspect of his life. He calculated carefully before taking risks. When he bought the ships that would eventually become profitable enough for his father to buy, he'd chosen routes that were lucrative, but most importantly, that would not hesitate at a half-Chinese ship captain.

His philosophy had made him rich. It had proven its efficacy again and again, and Edward dutifully applied it in even the most miniscule situations.

Except one.

Falling in love with Persephone had not been a calculated choice. It had been a headfirst tumble that he'd had no chance of stopping. Just like seeing her again in that ballroom. What he felt for her was beyond reason.

Reason had motivated his choice to break off their engagement. He could not bear the tears in her eyes when she'd recounted the social snubs. They'd started off small—a missed invitation, a friend who did not return her letter. Then they grew, culminating in the Countess of Tilbury giving her the cut direct. That was when he realized their relationship was doomed. The *ton* would not accept a poor man with his heritage.

But he was not a poor man any longer. No one would spurn

Persephone for being courted by him, not when so many of the ton's lords had reaped such profit from their investments in Johns Maritime Enterprises.

It was no longer the *ton* that might reject him.

It was that Persephone would.

She was the only thing in the world worth the risk.

But he could not be thinking of her as he entered *La Rose Rouge*. It did not seem right.

He didn't bother to doff his hat as he entered the brothel.

The brawny guard at the inner door did not react to his presence at all. Edward hated that he'd learned to expect as much, and often settled for less. But this visit was not about his pride.

He had another need to satiate tonight.

"Bonjour, Monsieur Johns."

He barely glanced at the fake French Madame as his foot hit the first stair.

"Madeline," he said over his shoulder. "My usual room."

He received a string of garbled pseudo-French words in response, but he didn't pause to decipher them.

They had an understanding, he and the Madame. He paid her an obscene amount of money, and she ensured none of her girls commented on his parentage. Quite ironically, it was the courtesans, rather than the ladies of the *ton*, who were more likely to show derision for his heritage. In a place like this, they could afford to be selective about their clientele. But the women who threw themselves at his feet in Mayfair ballrooms had decided he was worth their interest despite—or because of—his appearance.

He had not wanted for female companionship in a long time. The term rake was honestly applied in his case. But he'd still found himself at brothel time and again. The interaction was different, when there was money involved. Less talking. Less artifice. Less need for him to be perfect.

He walked by rote to a room on the first floor, tucked into the back corner abutting the mews. An easy scramble out the window if he ever had need.

Before the door had clicked behind him, he'd already yanked his cravat free. The silk cascaded silently into the discarded topper. Greatcoat. Tailcoat. Waistcoat.

A thick pile of expensive fabrics on a trunk at the foot of the bed.

Edward was pouring his second glass of wine when the door creaked open behind him.

"Monsieur—"

The young woman froze as he turned. She stumbled back a step, catching herself on the doorframe.

"Not the Monsieur Johns you were expecting."

His brother's favorite harlot blushed scarlet from the edges of her barely concealed areolas all the way to her crown of golden hair.

He could understand the appeal. She was still young enough to be fresh-faced; lacking the resignation the others hid with varying degrees of success.

"Your pardon, Monsieur," the young woman—Madeline—said, stepping back into the room with a forced smile. She looked ready to dart out of the room, even as she managed to get herself back over the threshold. Edward vaguely wondered what had made her so skittish.

The Madame gave all her girls French names. It had never occurred to Edward to wonder what one of their real names might be.

Madeline tugged nervously at the ribbon holding her sheer dressing gown in place. But Edward shook his head, knocking back another glass of wine as she paused in confusion.

"When was the last time you saw Alfred?" he asked without preamble.

Madeline swallowed, her throat bobbing in the low light from the singular candelabra, but she did not speak. Her eyes darted to the door.

Edward opened the small purse he'd dropped next to the wine bottle and dumped its contents onto the table shoved against the wall. Bed, trunk, table. All various heights for varied fucking.

The innocence dimmed in Madeline's eyes as the coins spilled out.

"Alfred?" he reminded her.

Her tongue darted out over her lips.

"Just after the new year," she said, her eyes never leaving the table.

"How long after?"

She blinked. "I do not recall, exactly."

Edward covered the pile with his palm. "Try harder."

The young woman blinked a few times, eyes refocusing on him.

"Epiphany," she said. "I remember the bells chiming just as we—"

"That's enough." He slid the pile across the table and stalked back toward the bed, where the window was closed tightly against the cold.

He suddenly felt the desperate need to throw it open, just to feel the sting on his face. It felt wrong to even be here, knowing that Persephone was in London. Knowing what he wanted from her. For her. With her.

"You are most generous, Monsieur," Madeline said, finally done collecting her due.

Edward issued a non-committal sound of dismissal, his mind already fitting this new information into the timeline he'd constructed of the days leading up to Alfred's disappearance. He would find Persephone tomorrow and tell her what he'd learned, to glean if she had any new information. And hopefully find some excuse to touch her again.

"How else may I be of service this evening?" the courtesan said, her words slipping uninvited between his thoughts.

He glanced her way. She'd struck a seductive pose, but it was tense. Her eyes still straying back to the door. She had one hand on her hip, attempting to emphasize her shapely curves.

Not shapely enough.

Dark curls and soft, rounded curves filled his memory, his fantasies.

"Go," he said softly.

She toyed with the edge of her dressing gown, then opened her mouth as if she wanted to speak. But the command in his face was enough, sending her retreating without further question. He locked the door behind her.

Edward's forehead dropped forward against the door with a *thump*.

He'd just paid a small fortune to sleep alone in a brothel.

He groaned and let his hand drop to his trousers. One woman rose to his mind as he reached for his cock. And it certainly wasn't the courtesan who'd just departed.

Chapter Nine

Persephone unfolded the packet carefully—to avoid spilling even a single confection—and promptly popped one of the gumdrops into her mouth. But even that was not enough to avoid Madison's questioning.

"This is how you want to spend your time? Writing thank you notes?" Madison asked dubiously, even though they were already *en route* to Lady Wheeler's townhouse.

Persephone refolded the packet of sweets and tucked them into her reticule before answering. "The Charity League for Orphans is a very worthy enterprise, and if this small gesture on my part helps in the raising of funds, then I am more than happy to divert an afternoon."

One corner of Madison's mouth quirked in an expression of outright disbelief. But she did not question her any further.

"Shall we work out some sort of distress signal for if the other needs rescuing?" she said instead.

Persephone nearly choked on the gumdrop.

Madison's mouth graduated to a full smile. "Feigning a swoon is too obvious. We'll be suspected immediately. My sisters and I used to have a whole assortment of bird whistles for when we wanted out of lessons, supper, and so on. But that won't do in a salon with nary an open window in January..."

"We could say 'My heavens, I've forgotten to post that letter to my brother!'" Persephone suggested, the previously ridiculous notion beginning to have appeal. If she needed to make a quick exit to relay information to Edward, or corner a particular lady to question her about her ransom-note-writing, it could be quite useful.

Madison grinned. "Except that I do not have a brother."

"And I do not have a sister," Persephone laughed.

"Mother, then. It will sound more urgent, in any case. Mothers always seem to think that timely correspondence from their daughters is directly indicative of their wellbeing," Madison decreed. And just in time, because the carriage was coming to a stop.

Lady Wheeler's home had been transformed overnight. Gone were the rows of chairs from the previous evening's auctions, replaced with a variety of tables, each outfitted with luxe linens and scrumptious tea services. Persephone paused to wonder where she'd obtained so many sets, and if she'd purchased them specifically for this afternoon's writing.

Of course, along with the tea and cakes and savories were thick stacks of creamy paper and sharpened quill pens standing at the ready. The writing of thank you notes was the necessary excuse for an afternoon of gossiping and angling for position in the upcoming season.

Madison departed her side with a quick squeeze of her arm, smiling and waving to a pretty woman with dark blonde curls on the other side of the sitting room.

There were no place cards, which Persephone took to mean that she could take any seat. But she lingered by the window instead, pretending to examine a tropical potted plant on a stand. While she could not be sure, she guessed she was looking for a younger lady. The grand dames of the *ton* would not be writing ransom notes. It was, however, the sort of thing an impressionable young lady might do at the behest of a less-than-reputable lover.

She marked the table she wanted a few minutes later. In the far corner of the room, seven seats were occupied by women who had mostly come in tow with their mothers, a few with elder sisters. Which left one seat open for her.

Persephone angled her body through the crowded sitting room.

"Lady Persephone, won't you join us?"

She bit down hard on her tongue to keep in the curse.

"What a kind invitation," she said as she turned, sweeping her gaze over the occupants of the table nearest her.

A few she recognized, a few she did not. A smattering of ages. Wives, mostly. Miss Dawson was still unmarried, bordering on spinsterhood. Lady Emberly had been widowed for most of Persephone's life.

She was about to decline when the latter nodded to the last remaining empty chair. "Do join us," Lady Emberly said more firmly this time.

Persephone accepted her lot with a graceful smile, sinking into the seat and folding her ankles under the table. She nodded at the women she knew and accepted introductions to the ones she did not.

"Lady Persephone, how lovely that you were able to join us," Lady Emberly commented as she handed out the lists of donors stacked neatly beside the teapot. She'd self-appointed herself the secretary of their table, it seemed.

"The marchioness was already planning to attend, so it was no trouble at all," she said, accepting her list and scanning the names. "How thorough Lady Wheeler is," she added.

"Indeed," Lady Emberly said. "I do wonder who will be writing the note of thanks to your Mr. Johns."

Persephone did not miss the slight twist of the older woman's mouth. Not a smile, but a grimace.

"He is hardly *mine*." Though the words were bitter in her mouth.

She forced herself to begin writing the first note, while also covertly trying to sneak glances at the other women as they picked up their quill pens. She'd forced Edward to bid for expensive horses he did not need so she could gain entrance to this event, where a large group of women would all be writing. If she had any luck at all, a few of them would be left-handed.

Lady Emberly was using her right. Not a surprise, though she seemed the type to hold someone for ransom. Mrs. Dupree used her left, but she was a middle-aged mother of four who Persephone had never heard speak louder than a whisper. Not a likely candidate.

"You see, Priscilla, it is as I said," Lady Emberly said to her daughter-in-law beside her. Persephone divided her attention between writing her note and watching the other women around her as covertly as she could. "The Duke would never allow his daughter to become involved with a man."

Anger, incandescent, unhinged, and not even tangentially related to her plan to find Alfred, speared though Persephone.

"Lady Emberly! I did not realize you were acquainted with my father!" she cried.

The woman rotated in her seat, thick gray hair catching the afternoon sunlight and turning to steel to match her gaze.

Persephone did not flinch.

"I came out in the same season as his sister," Lady Emberly said. "A different time, that was. A different century. One could not buy their way into a function as they can now."

The irony was not missed on Persephone as her hand stilled on the half-finished note to a donor.

How dare the woman say such things. If Persephone truly had been courting with Edward—but she wasn't.

But these ladies could never know that.

That was the reason for her sharp response. Not because she

actually cared about Edward after all of these years.

"Better an impoverished marquess than a self-made king?" Persephone said.

The other woman had the grace to color beneath her layers of pale powder. But Persephone was not satisfied. Not when she'd insulted Edward. The entire Johns family. His grandfather was a duke, for heaven's sake.

The implied slight at her was nothing. Persephone wanted to solve problems for the genteel ladies of the *ton* and find a kind, amiable husband. This dour old lady would not help her achieve either of those goals.

She handed her list to the woman sitting beside her, preparing to push out her chair.

"You must be quite accomplished, having spent so many years in New York. Do tell us everything you learned," Lady Emberly said, her lips a thin line of disapproval.

As if a decade abroad could be summed up in a single conversation.

But Persephone smiled indulgently as she finished the note she'd been writing with a graceful flourish. "Americans are delightfully forthcoming. You never have to wonder at what they are thinking because they simply say it."

"A habit you admired?"

"Naturally! Imagine how much simpler our days would be if we simply said what we were thinking rather than intimating it." She offered Lady Emberly a smile dripping with sweetness that even a mouthful of her gumdrops could not have matched. "If you'll excuse me. I shall go see if there is another group that needs my assistance."

It took every bit of self-control and decorum her mother had taught her to keep the smile in place as she turned away. When all she really wanted to do was kick that chair right out from underneath Lady Emberly.

The nerve of the woman—

"Oh, my heavens!"

"Zounds! I—"

Persephone clutched the back of a chair to keep herself upright. Thankfully, it was occupied, otherwise her buxom body would have been more than sufficient to send both her and the piece of furniture tumbling.

As it was, she was mostly unrumpled, although her heart was racing. The poor young woman she'd crashed into was not as lucky.

"Oh, my heavens," Persephone said again, pressing down the sigh in her chest. She was unmarked. But the stack of thank-you letters the young woman had been carrying was covered in ink from the inkpot she had also been carrying. Until Persephone upended it.

"Please forgive me. I've made an utter mess of your hard work, Miss..."

"Miss Bradshaw. Elizabeth Bradshaw," the younger woman supplied. She was blinking down at her stack of papers as if still trying to make sense of what had happened.

"Let me help you," Persephone said gently, easing the inkpot out of her hand and setting it on the nearest table, whose occupants leaned far out of the way.

Then she reached for the sheaf of papers. The top several were ruined, but perhaps the one or two at the back were intact.

Persephone's heart stopped.

One beat.

Two.

Then it started beating again and dozens of thoughts cascaded through her mind all at once.

The young woman—Elizabeth—had clutched everything in her left arm. The slant of the writing, the exaggerated loop on the letter *d* and the curled flourish at the end of each line. It was her. She was the one—

"My heavens, I've forgotten to post that letter to my mother!"

Chapter Ten

Madison chose to stay on, having found her friend Harriet, Viscountess Bayfield, also in attendance. It was a simple, if winding carriage ride back to the Warsham's residence. Persephone hardly needed a chaperone for the endeavor.

She scarcely noticed the driver who handed her up into the carriage, closing the door securely behind her.

Her mind was already spinning with possibilities.

Miss Bradshaw had looked at her as if she was daft when she proclaimed loudly about the need to post a letter to her mother—as did everyone else in attendance. But it was enough of a distraction to shove the last piece of paper from the otherwise spoiled stack into her pocket.

She'd need the ransom note to convince Edward, surely, but Persephone was already certain.

Miss Bradshaw. Elizabeth Bradshaw. Elizabeth.

She was in her second season, which meant she was still in the schoolroom when Persephone had left for America. But the name... Bradshaw... a brother. Two elder brothers, Persephone recalled. She could not summon their names, though she could picture them in her mind. The elder had thick blonde hair, a wide build, and was of an age with her. The other was younger by a few years. Lanky and with slightly darker hair. She wished she could remember anything about them other than their physical appearances.

It happened so fast, she did not even think about the motions as she executed them.

One moment, she was drumming her fingers on the stiff cushioned bench seat, the next she was thrown backward, her hand reaching for her skirts and grasping wildly.

She had the penknife out of her boot, into her hand, swinging wildly.

Then it was knocked free. Easily. Too easily.

She had to fight, she had to scream—

"Hush, or you'll doom us both," Edward said as he covered her mouth with his hand.

Persephone's first instinct was to bite it.

The second was to bite it, then drag her tongue over it, then suck on it.

Heavens. Maybe he'd knocked the sense right out of her.

He'd thrown himself into the carriage, sending her sprawling back against the wall. Her skirts were hiked up past her knees— she'd done that herself in her rush to get the pen knife her father had given her the day she'd departed for New York.

But she was not thinking about her father or New York or the whereabouts of the little jeweled knife.

She could not think at all.

Not with Edward's chest pressed against hers, that solid wall of steel caging her in, sliding against her nipples with every exhalation. She might as well have been naked for all the good the layers of her undergarments and pelisse did to stop the friction, the burning that was slowly snaking through every limb and inch of her body.

His knee was on the floor of the carriage, his arms thrown

wide to catch himself. And his lips—his beautiful, full lips, were right at her eye level.

All it would have taken was a lift of her chin, and they'd be there. Together, again. Just like before, just like she'd dreamed about for years.

"I beg your pardon," Edward said stiffly, heaving himself backward and sinking into the opposite corner of the bench seat while the carriage splashing through puddles and divots.

Persephone blinked rapidly, trying to clear her head. The thoughts were coming too fast now, colliding with feelings and making a terrible muddle of everything.

He'd jumped into Madison Warsham's carriage while the damn thing was rolling down the streets. What if he'd been seen? What if he'd *killed* himself?

She smacked him sharply across the knee with as much force as she could muster. "Have you taken leave of your senses? The driver—"

"Did not even notice. He merely thought he'd gone over a pothole," Edward said. He stared at the spot where she'd hit him with a strange, puzzled look on his face. Then he shook his head and looked back up at her, as if nothing strange had happened at all. "He and the footman are engaged in an argument of some kind."

Persephone had not even realized there was a footman. A poor bit of observation for the Lady Fixer of New York.

She curled her fingers into her palm to still the urge to hit him again. "And what will he think when we arrive at the Warsham's home and there are two occupants in the carriage instead of one?"

Edward shrugged. "I will be gone by then."

"And you are certain he will not notice your departure either, I assume." She shook her head, knowing she would not get an answer.

Even sitting as far from her as possible, Edward was broad, muscular, a man who took up space simply by existing. And in the close confines of the carriage... Persephone exhaled a shaky breath and tried to scoot a bit further away. But her back was already pressed against the wall. Any further, and she'd be dangling out the window. She didn't think even the distracted driver would miss that.

She did reach back and tug the window down a few inches, letting the cold air slip down the back of her pelisse to cool her neck, which was uncomfortably burning.

"What if Lady Warsham had been in here?" she exhaled, even though the argument was moot at this point.

"I saw you leave alone." Edward was leaning over, mucking about on the floor.

"You are following me." She hated the little flutter in her heart. His actions had nothing to do with her and everything to do with Alfred. Her stupid heart should not make any more of it than that.

"We are running out of time. I merely wished to make myself available in the case that you have information to share." He straightened, holding out his palm.

Her pen knife.

Persephone pursed her lips.

"Do you?" he pressed.

"Yes," she said tightly. She snatched back the knife, but instead of returning it to her boot and exposing her leg—she'd only just repositioned her skirts—she put it into the same pocket where she'd shoved the letter.

Which she took out and dropped onto the scant few inches of space on the bench seat between them.

"What is it?" Edward said, even as he picked it up and scanned. He lifted his brows when he reached the end of a tepid thank you note for a donation to the Charity League for Orphans.

"Do you have the ransom note with you?" she asked.

He hesitated—probably not keen to reveal where he'd put it

in case she decided to nick it again—but then withdrew the neatly folded paper from the inside breast pocket of his greatcoat.

"Look more closely at the handwriting." Persephone did not need to do so herself. She was already certain. But she did enjoy watching the recognition and understanding light in Edward's dark eyes.

"Who is Elizabeth Bradshaw?" he asked, handing her back the note. His hand lingered there to ensure it did not bounce out of his hand on the rough road. Not because he had any desire to touch her, surely.

"A left-handed young woman who was somehow convinced to write that ransom note. She has two elder brothers. I would wager that one of them, or both, has some connection to Alfred." She smiled smugly—until his brow creased with worry rather than triumph.

"What is it?" But before she'd finished that thought, another tumbled out as her mind hazarded a guess. "You know something as well."

Edward shifted in the seat, curling his hands into his lap—away from her. Why did that strike her as odd? Persephone's mind began sifting through possibilities, trying to see the connections. He was tense, that much was obvious. But why... why was he drawing away?

Because ever since he'd proposed their agreement, every action had been to reach *for* her. Not pull away.

But that could not be.

Why would he do that? He was the one who had broken things off between them.

"I do," Edward finally said, interrupting the maelstrom of thoughts in her mind.

Persephone stared at him expectantly, not trusting herself with words.

"I believe the last person to see Alfred before he disappeared was a harlot at the *La Rose Rouge*," he said.

Persephone's stomach flipped. "And you found this out by going to *La Rose Rouge?*"

"Yes."

Her stomach threatened to dump its contents right onto the carriage floor.

Every bit of warmth and foolish hope that had kindled inside of her died a sudden, painful death.

Of course. He couldn't satisfy himself by chasing down ladies of the *ton* while keeping up their pretense. But he could certainly turn to a whorehouse. Even if he was spotted, it would be dismissed as his due.

Men were always given that sort of freedom.

While women...

"What else?" she said, digging her fingernails into the velvet of the seat and staring at the paper in his hand. If she stared at him, she did not think she'd be able to restrain herself. "What else did your whore tell you?"

Edward's legs shifted position. "She is not my whore. She does not *belong* to anyone. I would have thought you of all women would protest the notion of—"

"Do not pretend like you know me." She ripped the note she'd stolen from Miss Bradshaw from his hand and tucked it back into her pocket. "Not anymore."

Silence reigned between them. Persephone wanted to look out the window, to mark her surroundings and estimate how many more minutes until she could be free of him. But that would require looking up, meeting his gaze, seeing the pity in his eyes. She just could not bring herself to do it.

"Ask what you really want to know, Persephone," Edward said quietly.

He shifted again, but this time, it was not just his legs. His whole body moved—closer, closer, until those scant inches of space between them disappeared altogether.

"Ask me if I spent the night with her," he breathed, mere inches from her now.

She was trembling. She could feel it. Edward could surely see it.

Maybe it was pity that made him say, "I slept alone last night. She's my brother's favorite, not mine."

It was certainly insanity which had her whispering, "Do you have a favorite?"

"There's only ever been one woman for me."

She understood what he meant. Not one woman in his bed—but one woman in his heart.

She wished he hadn't said it, at the same moment that her heart nearly exploded at the words. Because it meant that he was as affected as she. That even through the years, he had never stopped—

No.

It meant nothing.

Nothing had changed.

She'd opened her heart to Edward once, and he'd thrown it back at her. She would not make that mistake again.

"We are out of time." He was so close. Not inches anymore, but fractions of them. A jolt of the carriage and his mouth would be pressed against hers. It was all wrong, yet Persephone knew that the moment his lips touched hers she would be powerless to resist him.

But it was not his lips that touched hers.

It was his forehead. Pressed against hers, just for a moment. Less than that. The shadow of a moment.

Then he was gone.

Cold air rushed in from the opened and closed carriage door. A shiver shook her. And what Persephone wanted more than anything in the world, in that moment, was for Edward to be beside her once again, holding her tight against him, keeping her warm and safe.

Chapter Eleven

adison had been shockingly easy to convince. She apparently loved to host *ton* functions in her sprawling Mayfair mansion. Persephone did not question her luck. She merely provided a list of ladies she hoped to become better acquainted with, Madison added a few guests of her own, and the invitations for tea went out.

Every single one was accepted. Another advantage of being chaperoned by the most scandalous but also one of the most beloved hostesses of the *ton*.

When the Warsham's butler began showing in visitors, Persephone was ready.

As she watched Madison welcome their guests, she understood why the woman was so popular despite her unconventionality. With her golden hair loose around her shoulders, her effervescent smile, and her effusively kind words for every person who entered, it was so very easy to see why everyone loved the Marchioness of Clydon.

Once guests began settling in for tea, three-tiered trays began arriving, and Madison made her way over to introduce her two sisters. Leonora and Meera, one older and one younger. Persephone smiled and exchanged pleasantries, but her eyes swept relentlessly over the guests, waiting for Miss Bradshaw's arrival.

Which was how her eye caught the flash of green in the hand of another woman who'd been on the list she'd handed over to Madison days ago.

Making her excuses to Madison and her sisters, Persephone angled across the room to where the elderly Miss Ingram had just lowered herself to sit in the window, her cane resting against her knee.

"This reticule is so lovely," Persephone exclaimed, claiming the other half of the window seat with a wide smile.

"Thank you! Green has always been my favorite color." The spinster returned her genuine smile, bright and kind. In Persephone's experience, they tended to be one of two types—bitter about their circumstance and equipped with fangs, or perfectly happy and resigned to the life they'd chosen.

Thankfully, Miss Ingram appeared to be the latter. It made the rest of the plan she'd formed in her mind as she crossed the room so much easier.

"Mine as well!" Persephone said emphatically, motioning down at the green-embroidered day dress she'd selected with exactly this exchange in mind. "Miss Anna Winlock was describing one just like it to me, but she mentioned that hers has gone missing."

Realization dawned on the woman's face.

There was no artifice, no ill intent. Just the realization that she'd made a very embarrassing mistake.

"Are you well?" Persephone asked gently.

She watched the elderly woman's throat bob. "I think I may have accidentally pilfered Miss Anna's reticule when I was at her sister's at-home a few weeks ago. I have one very similar to it myself, you see." The mortification was coming off her in waves. "My sight is not what it once was—"

Persephone grasped her hand. She would not make this sweet

89

lady feel bad for an honest mistake. She could complete her task and leave Miss Ingram with her pride intact. It was one of the simplest resolutions to a task Persephone had ever experienced.

"Leave it with me," she told her, excusing herself for a few minutes.

When she returned, she pressed one of her own reticules, also a lovely bright green, into the older woman's hands.

"You may borrow this one of mine for your things, and I will see the other returned to Miss Anna. I will not even mention your name," she explained.

Miss Ingram's lip wobbled, but she did not let a tear fall. She gripped Persephone's hand as she accepted the second reticule. "You are a darling," she exclaimed.

Persephone merely smiled, asking about the inlaid details on Miss Ingram's cane as she unobtrusively helped her switch the contents of the reticule.

She was listening to the second story about Miss Ingram's niece, Henry, who'd gifted her the cane, when Elizabeth Bradshaw arrived.

Persephone remained in place, tracking the young woman with her eyes now and then, but trying not to be too obvious about it. Only when Miss Ingram had been joined by her sister, Henry's mother, and Elizabeth Bradshaw had finished her cup of tea, did Persephone approach.

"Miss Bradshaw, how lovely to see you again." She dipped a curtsey, but did not move to sit beside her on the sofa.

"Lady Persephone." Elizabeth stood, setting aside her empty teacup so she could curtsey as well. "You must extend my thanks to the marchioness for the invitation."

"I will, of course." Persephone waited, letting a beat of silence hang between them, before, "Have you visited the Warsham's home before?"

A quick shake of the head.

"Perhaps you'd allow me to show you some of the rooms?

The view of the gardens is spectacular, even in the winter," she offered.

Miss Bradshaw cast her gaze around the room, looking very much like she'd appreciate an escape. But it was well-known that Persephone was a guest of the marchioness, a hostess by proxy, and Elizabeth knew better than to be rude. Elizabeth's mother was drinking tea with an elderly woman that Persephone did not recognize. But from the slight wrinkle of Elizabeth's nose, she did not seem keen to join them.

"If you like," she finally agreed.

"Lovely!" Persephone looped arms with the other young woman, ignoring her arched brows, and led her from the parlor.

Through the grand foyer with its impressive sweeping staircase and massive glass chandelier. Past the empty ballroom that could easily have held hundreds, but that afternoon was shadowed and quiet. Beneath the arched windows of the atrium at the rear of the mansion that overlooked the impressive grounds, unusual to find in the middle of London.

Elizabeth nodded and offered short responses to Persephone's mindless chatter.

When they were far away from the other guests and had taken enough turns that Elizabeth would require her help to find her way back, Persephone stopped.

"I must admit to another motive, asking you along," she said, dropping her hands in front of her, wringing them. She'd had enough awkward conversations as the Lady Fixer to not be nervous about this one. But she also knew how to make herself appear nervous, to get the reaction she wanted.

Elizabeth sighed heavily. "Are you interested in one of my brothers?"

Persephone let her genuine surprise show. "No, nothing like that—well, perhaps." She paused, reached for her pocket, stopped, reached again. She huffed a dramatic little sigh. "May I show you something?"

Miss Bradshaw looked extremely uncomfortable. Which was precisely what Persephone wanted—an honest reaction.

"I promise, I do not bear you any ill will. It is only that I need your help, you see, and I, well, here." She thrust the ransom note into the other woman's hands.

If she'd had any doubts about whether Elizabeth had written the note, they died in that moment. The color leached from the young woman's face, her knuckles turning bright white where they clutched the note.

Still, in order to keep up her ruse, Persephone asked. "Did you write it?"

Elizabeth Bradshaw very much did not want to answer.

But Persephone remained silent.

"Yes," Elizabeth said, shoving the note back into Persephone's hand. As if she could not bear it and the culpability it implied. "But it was a jape. My brothers were playing a trick on a friend. I did not know—" Horror dawned on her face. "Is this Mr. Johns related to the Mr. Johns who escorted you to Lady Wheeler's auction?"

"I am afraid so." She clasped Elizabeth's hand in sympathy, just as she had with Miss Ingram in the parlor. "I was so anxious to ask you, but when we crashed into one another and I saw your notes, I recognized the handwriting." After orchestrating it just so.

Persephone paused another moment. "I hope you'll forgive me. But Edward, I mean, Mr. Johns," she pretended to stumble over her words, ignoring that the blush came to her cheeks a bit too easily. "He is quite worried over his brother."

Elizabeth was now worrying her lower lip, eyes softening slightly. Persephone must look like a woman in love, desperate to impress her paramour, nervous and jittery. In need of assistance.

Elizabeth reached out a tentative hand and laid it on Persephone's arm. "I will tell you what I know."

She did. Her brothers coming to her, asking her to write the note, promising her an outing to Newmarket. Apparently Miss Elizabeth Bradshaw adored horses. The scheme they'd described, their laughing faces. Always laughing, always ready for a jest, Elizabeth said earnestly.

None of it sounded dangerous. The way that Elizabeth described the interaction, it felt like it really was nothing more than a jape. A few mates up to a bit of fun. Did the Bradshaw brothers know Alfred? They must. They frequented a tavern in the docks to play cards, Elizabeth had said. Perhaps they had met Alfred there. But why would they wish him ill? Were they friends playing a prank? Edward certainly did not believe the ransom note to be a prank. If so, he never would have asked for her help. And Alfred truly *was* missing.

Elizabeth sniffed. "I wish I had never done it. Those gits have not even taken me to Newmarket as they promised."

Those gits. That was Persephone's thought exactly.

Chapter Twelve

The sun was already long set when Persephone finally climbed the stairs to her bedroom. Sitting through the afternoon of tea and frivolity was torturous when all she wanted to do was call the carriage and go find Edward. But even she wasn't quite bold enough to abandon so many important ladies and go alone to call on an unmarried man in a hotel.

As soon as their guests departed, Madison had swept her into the dining room for a casual supper with the family. They hadn't even gone up to change for the meal. Madison and her sisters were just so happy to be together. It should have made an easy opportunity for Persephone to excuse herself.

Yet she found herself lingering in the parlor long after the meal had concluded, unable to tear herself away from the tableau. If Madison was bold, her sister Meera was absolutely brazen. She laughed louder, smiled wider, and seemed to give voice to every thought as it entered her head. Leonora, elder by more than a decade, was quieter, holding her namesake on her lap and giggling softly. Her own belly was softly rounded with the middle stages of pregnancy.

The whole scene had Persephone sighing and hoping and wishing.

Only when the nurse appeared and escorted a drowsy Nora upstairs did Persephone finally extricate herself.

Each step up the stairs was a thought.

She wanted that.

Family, affection, happiness.

Love.

Her foot hit the landing.

Edward.

She needed to write to Edward, tell him what she'd found out.

Edward.

He was every beat of her heart, every dream she wouldn't let herself remember.

She could not want him.

A life with Edward... it would be more than passing affection. It would be all-consuming love, the sort that she'd seen with Madison and Henry, the kind she'd read about in novels. It would be warm embraces and kisses in the early morning light, long afternoons spent tangled in one another on the settee. Quiet moments in the shipping office, poring over manifests.

In a second, she could see it all. Right down to the dark-haired children that would play at their feet, building forts among the crates at the company's dockside warehouse and laughing in their grandparents' arms.

But it was all a mirage.

Edward might still hold feelings for her—he did still hold feelings for her. She forced herself to admit it, no matter how painful. But what were those feelings, precisely? What was there was more than lust... but was it love? And did it even matter if it was?

Loving one another had never been the problem.

For hours, she'd fought the pressing need to run up to her room and write to him, telling him all she'd learned, proposing about their next step. They had to find a pretense for speaking with the Bradshaw brothers. No doubt that was something Edward could accomplish without her. But she was too invested in saving Alfred to let him seek out valuable information on his own. Which was to say nothing of the two more social outings he still owed her.

Owed her?

She had not wanted him anywhere near her. Did not, she tried to correct herself.

But the protest rang false even in her own mind.

She should write to him, find Alfred, and dismiss him from their agreement. The charity auction coupled with their names mentioned together in *The Rake Review* column would have to be sufficient, if she had any hope of surviving the week without having her heart broken again.

But as she crossed her threshold, Persephone flinched away from the little writing desk tucked in the corner.

She let the maid who appeared help her undress, but dismissed her as soon as her nightgown was on and combed out her own hair. Others rarely knew how to tame her wild curls.

Then she plaited it.

And unplaited it.

She could not send the note until the morning, in any case. If she asked, she knew that Madison and Henry would send out a servant to deliver her missive to the hotel, even though it was past dark. They most likely would not press her for details.

But she might need their goodwill more on another night. Who knew what would be required as she and Edward came closer to uncovering the kidnapping plot.

She took out her little notebook instead, settling herself onto the bed rather than at the writing desk. Flipping through the pages, she avoided the ones where she'd sketched out ideas about Edward's motivations or Alfred's potential whereabouts. She looked over her notes on Miss Anna Winlock's reticule, added a few lines at the bottom to indicate how the task had been resolved. Then on to Lady St. James's son and his mistress. She'd paid Madison's kitchen maid a few coins to speak with her counterpart from the St. James household at the market, but the young woman had not reported back yet. She could try a different approach, but it really was not necessary. The task was proceeding nicely.

There was quite literally nothing left for Persephone to do other than write the note or go to sleep.

Damn.

She forced herself into the chair at the writing desk, pulled out a fresh sheet of stationary, wrote Edward's name, and then set the quill pen down.

Why?

Why was this seemingly simple task suddenly monumental?

Because every step toward finding Alfred was another step away from Edward, her heart answered.

Her foolish, traitorous heart.

The crystal clock over the mantle ticked away, second after second. The fire in the hearth still blazed, warming the entire room. If she delayed long enough, she'd still be awake when the maid came in to bank it for the night.

Tick. Beat. Tick. Beat.

Her heart competed with the clock for dominance in her ears.

They both marched on, no matter what she did. Whether she wrote the letter now or in an hour.

Persephone picked up the quill pen.

One sentence. Then another. The third was still a struggle, but the fourth came easier. One more. Then she was signing her name. Blowing on the ink to dry it, unable to look at the words.

Tick. Beat. Tick. Beat.

She folded it into a neat quarto, drizzled the wax, pressed in the seal.

But she did not set it down.

She stared at the curved edges of the wax where they'd bled

out from the force of the metal seal. She stared at the name she'd written on the front.

Then she lifted it to her mouth and pressed her lips to the elegant letters of his name.

Perhaps it was the last kiss they would ever share.

Chapter Thirteen

"You should not be here," Edward said for at least the hundredth time.

Here being a dockside tavern, at night, full of rowdy sailors and dockworkers who would be described as rough on their very best day.

Two days had passed since Elizabeth Bradshaw's confession to Persephone. It had taken that long for her to get word to Edward, and then for him to ask the employees at Johns Maritime Enterprises very discreetly where his brother liked to play cards—without his father hearing of it.

Two days remained until the ransom was due. Edward felt the time ticking away like a constant, physical pain. The situation with his brother would explode if they did not find him soon. Paying the sort of money demanded in the ransom note would only be acceptable if Alfred truly was in danger. If their parents found out Alfred... Edward took a long drink of ale. Alfred's captors would be the least of his problems.

Two days left with Persephone. Plus two more social outings.

It was not enough. It would never be enough.

But none of it would matter if Persephone got herself into trouble in a dockside tavern.

"Here I am, and here I will stay," she said, planting her hand on the tabletop. "Unless you plan on trussing me up like a chicken and returning me to Mayfair."

Stubborn, willful, beautiful woman. "That is precisely what I want to do."

"Since that is out of the question, we ought to focus our energy on the more relevant task at hand."

He wanted to spank her, kiss her, and then kill her. In that order.

He could probably get away with the first two without causing much of a scene. Dockside taverns weren't known for being beacons of propriety. But attempting the last would surely get them kicked out.

The tavern owner would not have an objection to killing on a moral basis. None of the lowlifes in the place would. But the barkeep was smart enough not to allow it to happen on his premises.

All of those lowlifes—and the too-interested looks they kept casting in Persephone's direction, were the reason he needed to get her *out*.

Or Alfred wouldn't be the only problem he had to deal with. Spending time with her, no matter how strongly his heart demanded it, was not acceptable at the cost of her safety.

He tried a different approach. "The marchioness will realize you are missing."

"She will not. I dismissed the maid for the evening and had her bank the coals in my room. I told her I wished to sleep late and not to disturb me before noon tomorrow. That is plenty of time to get back." He cast her a dubious look. "I also left Madison a note telling her not to worry."

Edward rolled his eyes up toward the low, scarred ceiling and muttered an oath.

"The Marchioness of Clydon may be lenient, but she is not unintelligent." He ought to be sending the marchioness flowers and gifts to thank her. If she'd been a proper chaperone, she'd never have allowed him so many chances with Persephone alone. *All those chances, and I still haven't kissed her.*

Persephone took a sip of the ale in front of her, wrinkling her nose as she set the tankard back down on the scarred wooden table. Her hand disappeared inside her cloak, emerging a second later to pop a barley sugar candy into her mouth.

"Even if she does suspect, she will not raise the alarm unless I fail to return by twelve o'clock tomorrow. I am certain of it," Persephone said as she sucked on the candy, her cheeks hollowing out in a way that had Edward's gut churning and his cock hardening.

She did *look* certain, no matter what she actually felt. Her arms were lazily crossed on the table top, her fingernail idly digging into one of the grooves in the wood. She'd plaited her dark hair and avoided any of the fripperies of the upper echelons where she normally spent her time.

She certainly did not fit in among the patrons of the tavern. She was too clean to be a resident of the dockside slums and too modestly clothed to be one of the women who worked the rooms upstairs. But she'd made a decent job of at least not calling extra attention to herself.

Edward knew it would only last for a finite amount of time.

Persephone might be clever enough to survive for a few hours, but Edward had grown up in taverns like this one. First in Portsmouth, then in London. It was places like this where his father recruited sailors and drank with his ship captains. He himself had rented a room in this very pub years ago when he was only in port for a few days. Before he had quarters of his own above the warehouse.

How different than the hotel amenities.

But the glances he received were the same.

Foreign, they said. *Not one of us*, they threatened.

No one would care that his grandfather was a duke before they began throwing punches.

He could stand them. He'd inherited his father's broad shoulders, had taken lessons in pugilism from the best that the *ton* had to offer. But while the gentleman of the *ton* sparred for sport in the ring, Edward had honed his skills in dark places such as this— or in the alleys behind them. Again, tavern owners rarely tolerated that sort of behavior inside their establishments. But once he stepped into the street, he was fair game.

And so was Persephone.

"We need to leave."

Persephone pinned him with a look that told him the only way he'd get her out of the tavern was if he threw her over his shoulder. And even then, she'd be kicking and screaming.

"We need to find the Bradshaw brothers and their friend, Tomlinson. Elizabeth said their card game is on Tuesday evenings, so they must be here somewhere." As she spoke, she scanned the other patrons.

She'd described the three young men to him, but as of yet they hadn't seen anyone enter the tavern matching the requirements.

"They will most likely be in a back room," Edward said. Which was why this hare-brained plan had been flawed to begin with. It would be easier to get the Bradshaw brothers talking in a tavern rather than a drawing room, with less polite manners of persuasion at his disposal. "If it's a closed game, it won't take place out here where anyone could try to join."

She tilted her head to the side, exposing the pale column of her throat and the three familiar freckles. Edward's mouth was suddenly very dry.

"Why would three noble gentlemen come to the docks to play cards?" she asked. "It seems unnecessarily dangerous."

She could acknowledge the danger of playing cards with

ribald sailors and dangerous lowlifes, but not the danger of sitting in a tavern drinking with them. *Fucking hell.*

"The danger is what draws them." Edward exhaled through his nose as he took a long drink of his own ale. Piss poor, watered down, and exactly what he needed to steady himself. He'd practically gone from mother's milk to tavern ale. He finished his own tankard, then reached for Persephone's.

"Why are men so stupid," she murmured under her breath.

"Says the unmarried daughter of a duke sitting in a dockside pub with the least marriageable man in London."

He waited for the barbed rejoinder, sucking down ale to cushion the blow.

But when Persephone's mouth opened, it wasn't to spar. Her lovely bow-shaped lips stretched into a wide smile, and then a deep, velvety chuckle that reached inside of him and filled all the empty, hollowed out places Edward hadn't even realized were there.

He let himself bask in it for a full minute.

Then he set down the empty tankard and reached for her hand. "They aren't here. Let's go find another disreputable tavern for you to sit in."

* * *

The second tavern was a disappointment as well.

But the ale softened him, just a bit, and Persephone's smile remained near the surface, and Edward could not remember the last time he'd felt quite so... happy.

The word was a balm and a wound to his soul. It could not last forever. But it was so incredibly sweet that he could not stop himself from savoring it, just for a few hours.

Yet as the hours dragged on, the clientele of the dockside drinking halls turned darker as well. When a large man nearly Edward's size and sporting a thick scar down his cheek actually tried to proposition her, going so far as to drop a shilling on the table in front of them, Edward knew their time was up.

He made sure that her pelisse was fully buttoned up, and the cloak she'd worn over it to conceal the fine fabric tied as well, before taking her by the arm and stepping into the frigid night.

"Where to next?" Persephone asked, her breath a puff of white mist even in the low light.

"Nowhere. It is after midnight. We need to get you back to Mayfair." Edward tightened his grip on her arm, half expecting her to bolt

Her brow furrowed, but she remained in place.

Small mercies.

"We haven't found them yet," she said.

Edward was only half listening. He was monitoring the street, the row of warehouses that began a few blocks down, looking to where the masts of ships would be visible in the daylight. He noted every beggar asleep against a doorway, every watering-hole and drunken sailor hanging out of it.

"I will come back another night," he said.

"But Elizabeth said they only play on Tuesdays. We cannot wait another week, the ransom note—"

"Demands I pay before then. I am well aware." What they would do next to find Alfred was not his concern in that moment; getting Persephone back to the safety of the Warsham's mansion was.

She chewed on her lower lip as he led her a few steps further down the street. "Why aren't you more concerned about Alfred? The ransom note promises bodily harm if the money is not paid. I've tried to explain it away, but no scenario quite fits."

"I am concerned about Alfred. But in this moment, I am more concerned about you being down here in the middle of the night." *Shit, shit, shit.* She was figuring him out. He did not have time for this. This argument had to wait until later.

There were no hackneys to be had. This area was too

dangerous for most of them; a driver was as likely to be stabbed and robbed as he was to find a fare on the docks so late at night. They would have to walk a few blocks, at least, before they found a conveyance. Even then, they would need to be on guard against bandits.

He mapped out the most well-lit path with his mind, then pulled Persephone flush against his side and started down it. Past two more taverns, then into an alleyway.

It was darker than he wanted, but there were at least residences on either side of it. Maybe they'd get lucky and there would be someone hanging up the wash or smoking their pipe. They were safer with more eyes upon them.

"Edward—" Persephone protested again.

"We need to find a hackney," he said.

But she yanked herself out of his grip, swinging around so she could see him fully. "There is something you do not want to tell me."

He did not cover his reaction fast enough. She saw the guilt in his eyes, as clearly as he saw the recognition in hers.

"We will talk about it later," he said, reaching for her arm.

But Persephone yanked hers away. "You've been lying to me. What... is the ransom note a fake? Is Alfred in any danger? He must be. Elizabeth believed it to be real. But why... why would you lie to me? Why would you trick me into spending all this time with you? You cannot... no, no, no."

It was the way her mind functioned, throwing out every possibility, tracking back and forth between actions and possible reactions. He'd seen her do it on a piece of paper, but with none to hand, she was speaking the thoughts aloud.

"Persephone." He reached for her again, trying to break through the storm cloud of thoughts swirling around her.

"Do not touch me!" she cried, stepping back.

Edward cringed, hand dropping. "I am sorry, I..." He swallowed the words, straining his ears to listen through the darkness.

Those were footsteps behind them.

"We have to go, *now.*" He reached for her again, hesitated. But Persephone had frozen, her eyes following the approaching sound into the darkness of the alley behind them.

They needed to reach the next street. There was a boarding house, a stable, and a brothel. Not ideal, but better than a dark alley.

The footsteps were speeding up. More than one. He tried to count the footfalls behind them, but they were coming too fast.

Persephone stumbled a step away, toward the street waiting at the other end of the alley. But they were out of time.

He threw his hand over her mouth, pulling her tight against him with his other arm and dragging her into against the wall, into the darkest pocket of shadow he could find. She was wiggling in his arms, but he did not dare lean down and whisper even a word of comfort in her ear. Not on the infinitesimal chance that he'd been wrong, that they hadn't been noticed...

The low click of a tongue, the sound someone used to admonish a wayward child, filled the surrounding shadows a second before the trio stepped into the light.

Persephone stilled.

Edward made his assessments quickly. The one at the front, the tallest of the three, the one clicking his tongue—he was their leader. But it was the man on his right, short and barrel-chested, the white scars visible on his bare hands, who would do the most damage. The third had a knife in his hand.

"Stay behind me," he murmured, maneuvering her slowly behind his wide frame.

It was too much to hope the motion would be unnoticed by the three men. Well-dressed enough not to live in the dockside slums, but coarse. From families with just enough money to make them feel entitled, superior. Dangerous.

"There's no need to hide from us, pet," the leader said,

cracking a charming smile at Persephone. "We've come to save you."

"I do not need saving," she said quickly.

"Be quiet," Edward hissed.

"You don't speak to her that way." The charm dripped away as his chin snapped back to Edward.

"Fucking animal," the burly man snarled, followed by a string of slurs so nasty, Edward had to grit his teeth to keep from reacting. He'd heard them all before. A hundred times. Maybe a thousand.

But Persephone had not.

She muffled her gasp, but Edward did not miss the way her fingernails dug into his bicep.

"You heard the lady. She is fine. Let us pass." Even as he said the words, Edward started angling his body, tensing his muscles. It was a feeble last attempt for Persephone's sake, but he knew what was coming.

"She would say that if she was afraid, would she not?" The man smiled again. "Come, my lady," he said, attempting a bow that spoke to his less than noble origins. If the sneer over the sobriquet had not been indication enough.

"I will not go with you." Persephone's voice was clear, strong. Not a shake or tremble, despite the fact that he could feel her heart hammering where her chest was pressed against his back.

"You sully yourself with him. A fine English rose, dragged through the filth." He cut a glance to his companions on either side of him. "We'll teach you how a proper Englishman does things."

Edward's restraint snapped.

He'd been a bowstring pulling taught from the moment he'd heard their footsteps. But the threat to Persephone loosed him. He was not the great-grandson of a duke or a half-member of the noblesse; there in the dark alley, he was brutal death.

He shoved Persephone toward the street at the other end of

the alleyway, still too far away. He didn't wait to see if she stumbled or kept her feet, or whether she decided to run or stay. He didn't give up his advantage.

Edward launched himself forward, throwing the full weight of his body into that first punch. The snarling leader dodged to the side, but he hadn't been the target. Edward curled one fist around the wrist of the tall man on the right, wrenching it until he dropped the knife, while he buried the other fist in the man's face.

Most men were either big or fast. Edward was both. He had to be both in order to survive in these alleys, long before he'd met Persephone.

Every high-browed English drunkard wanted a piece of the half-Chinese upstart who had the audacity to own so many of the ships anchored in the river. Wanted to teach him his place.

He'd learned it, too.

They wanted him to play the villain?

Fine. He had no problem making them bleed.

The tall man stayed down, grasping around him to try and find his lost knife. But Edward had already shoved the dagger into his own boot, even as he whirled for the burlier of the two men still standing. He dodged the fist of the leader, but the bull landed a jab to his stomach.

He doubled over, the air knocked out of lungs, but forced himself back up even as he dragged in a breath, trying to refill them. He couldn't expose his neck—too vulnerable. But he used the reaction of his body to draw the knife again.

The burly man leaned forward over him, ready to grab his head and snap his neck. Edward swung his head up hard, catching the other man in the chin and sending him staggering backward. He got his leg up just before the man was out of range, a boot straight to the bollocks.

Which left the leader. Snarling through a busted lip. Edward did not even recall giving it to him. He turned, knife raised, ready to slash—

But then his foot was being yanked out from under him. The man on the ground, the one whose knife he now grasped, was trying to pull him down.

Edward ducked, throwing one arm up to shield his head from the attacker above while he stabbed downward with the blade at the one below.

He'd get out of this, he knew he would. He always did. Bigger foes, better armed, bested again and again.

But never with Persephone on the fringes.

Every swing of his fist or swipe of the blade was buying her time to get away. To get to the end of the alleyway, to the relative safety of the lit street. She was smart. She'd be able to find her way back to Mayfair unharmed.

But the sneering leader had not forgotten her either. He started to turn, out of Edward's reach.

Then just as suddenly froze, bellowed, stumbled forward. Into Edward's range.

Edward didn't hesitate. He drove his fist up into the man's jaw, sending him sprawling backward, knocking Persephone back onto the ground as well.

Why was she there? What was she doing?

Edward stepped clear of the pile of limbs and blood. Then he saw the glint in the single shaft of moonlight—her jeweled penknife, buried in the man's shoulder.

If he'd been alone, only his life at risk, he might have laughed at the absurdity.

Instead he leaned down, yanking the penknife from the man's back with one hand—dodging the spurt of blood that followed as best he could. He reached for Persephone with the other.

He hauled her up, refusing to let the fear in her eyes register or he would turn around and murder the bastards. She took one step toward the street at the other end of the alley. A few more. Edward followed, her hand still in his.

She wasn't injured. Relief coursed through him.

Behind them, a low, ominous growl sounded through the darkness.

Edward nudged her into the street.

"Run."

Chapter Fourteen

Her boots were not made for running. Nothing about her was. Her chest was heaving, her thighs rubbed together under her gown, beginning to burn despite the frost that coated her lungs with each breath she dragged in.

She was going to die—not from the three villains that Edward had dispatched with brutal efficiency. From the ice crystals forming inside of her. Persephone was certain that if she wiped at her mouth, her hand would come away bloody.

But Edward pulled her along. Down the street, through another alley. She flinched—this one was darker than the last. Edward hauled her into it, never breaking step. A minute later, they were back on the street where they'd started. She recognized the tavern they'd stepped out of mere minutes before, and suddenly she wanted nothing more than to crawl back into its warmth.

Safety. It must be safe there, in the light, with all those people.

But the three men had followed them from the tavern. They must have. It wasn't any safer there than out on the street.

She opened her mouth to ask where they were going, but all that came out was a gasp. Edward did not react, even though he must have heard it. She'd seen him be calm and composed in the face of discrimination. But descending into this place of cool, brutal calculation was something different entirely. Maybe it ought to have scared her.

But as she ran with him along a row of towering warehouses, leaving behind the row of pubs and the respite of light and warmth, a deep intrinsic part of her knew he would do anything to keep her safe.

He skidded to a stop suddenly in front of one of the warehouses. In front of a door. He caught her arm to keep her upright as he turned her around, back the way they'd come.

"Watch," he ordered, while he dug around urgently inside his greatcoat. A second later, she heard the telltale scrape of metal on metal, followed by a wonderful, blessed, near-magical *click*.

He pulled her through the door with the same unflinching, efficient movements. Locked it behind her. Pushed her toward the stairs.

Stairs.

Persephone winced, her thighs already screaming in protest.

She thought of Edward, throwing his body at the three villains, one of them with a *knife*—all to save her. She forced herself up a step.

She could feel his warm presence behind her, a wall of strength. A promise of safety. She managed a few more stairs.

It was more than one flight, though there were no landings to break up the never-ending staircase. They were in a warehouse, she told herself. Was he taking her to the roof? Did he know of some other route that would take them over rooftops to safety?

Her stomach clenched. She'd never much cared for heights. Just looking out the attic window of her parents' townhouse growing up had made her queasy.

This time, when they reached the locked door, Edward did not tell her to watch. He merely nudged her aside on the small landing, using yet another key retrieved from inside his greatcoat.

The door swung open with a creak loud enough to set her teeth on edge. Whatever this place was, it had not been used lately. But for Edward to have not one key, but two... the warehouse must belong to Johns Maritime Enterprises.

While her mind ran in circles, Edward began lighting lamps.

It must be an office or a—

Bedroom.

Not only a bedroom, Persephone's addled mind admonished. Though the bed was what immediately drew her eye. There were two tall bookcases against the far wall. Nestled between them was a massive desk covered in neatly stacked ledgers and folios. A single armchair flanked the hearth. A washbasin tucked in the corner. Windows covered by heavy curtains lined one wall. The other housed a few shelves with basic cooking utensils, though it appeared any actual cooking must be done in the hearth itself.

But her eyes inevitably went back to the bed in the corner. It was narrow, meant for one. Not a place that Edward brought his conquests.

As Edward started removing layers and hanging them up on pegs near the hearth, she realized it was the opposite of a den of iniquity. This was his home.

There were touches of him everywhere, now that she looked for them. The extra pillow on the bed, because he thought that propping himself up helped with his snoring. The way the ledgers on the desk were stacked just so, to leave the clear working space his mind required when reviewing calculations. Even the cookware in the makeshift kitchen—a smaller version of the Chinese clay pot she'd once watched his mother use to cook.

Edward held out his hand for her cloak at the same time that she finished her survey of the one-room apartment.

"You live here," she said simply.

Edward's eyes narrowed for a moment, as if he was considering denying it. But then his brow smoothed, and he took her cloak, followed by the pelisse she'd buttoned beneath. "It is a safe place to hide until morning."

Persephone glanced back at the door to the stairs—locked once more—and shivered.

"I will get the hearth going," Edward said.

He bent over to do just that, and rather than allow herself to admire his backside, Persephone drifted toward the row of windows and peeked out behind the curtains. Outside was mostly darkness. Some light filtered up from the street below; lanterns outside of business warning would be intruders away, the glow through thick glass windows of the taverns that never really closed.

A group of men stumbled down the street and she immediately tensed. Of course, they were not the same villains who'd attacked them, their builds were all wrong, and they continued drunkenly right past their door.

She snapped the curtains shut.

Perhaps she was safer admiring Edward's muscular backside after all.

He was slowly adding kindling to the growing flame, watching to make sure it took solidly before adding the first thick log.

"It is a small room. It will heat up quickly," he said as he straightened—and avoided her eyes.

What could he possibly be embarrassed about? Or was that regret? He'd just saved her life, for heaven's sake.

Could it be the apartment? She'd just asked if it was his home, and then lapsed into silence.

"It is lovely," she said with complete honesty.

It was not ornate or luxurious. Those things did not impress her—she'd spent her whole life around them. It was the comfort of this place that appealed to her. The fact that everywhere she turned, she saw Edward in it. That alone made the apartment more beautiful to her than any grand palace.

"Why do you stay in the Pendleton, when you have this waiting for you here?" she asked, frowning.

Edward shrugged casually. When there was absolutely nothing casual about the tension building between them in this room. Where they would spend the night. With one tiny, narrow bed.

For their safety, of course.

"The *ton* has certain expectations," he said woodenly.

He pulled out a chair from the dining table, but waited to sit down until she'd moved to the armchair. She let herself sink into the heavily-cushioned wingback.

She settled herself back, crossing and uncrossing her legs, unable to dislodge the slight discomfort borne not of physical, but emotional turmoil.

"When did you become so concerned about appeasing the *ton*?" It was that change, more than anything else about him, that struck her after the last ten years. Money had never mattered to her. Neither had the lack of a title. She'd had both growing up and found that while they smoothed the way, they did not guarantee happiness.

Edward had plenty of money now. And he was generally accepted by the *ton*. It must have taken him every minute of the last ten years to achieve it. But she needed to know *why*.

He cleared his throat, the words sticking. "When the Countess of Tillbury gave you the cut direct at court."

As hard for him to say as it was for her to hear.

Persephone pressed her eyes shut. She did not want to remember.

"My father will not live forever," Edward continued, staring past her into the growing flame in the hearth. "I have to make the connections and bargains that come so easily to him."

Because his father looked like society's idealized version of an Englishman. While Edward did not.

"That is such utter shite," she said, smacking her palm down hard on the arm of the chair.

Edward's features were immovable. He stared into the fire. Then suddenly, he chuckled. A chuckle that spilled into a laugh. A sound so rare and precious that Persephone found herself basking in it, committing every detail of his face and body to memory so she might recall it later.

"It is shite. And every day, I wade through it," he finally said, straightening.

Persephone bit her lower lip. "I am sorry, Edward."

An apology for the world she'd been born into, which was so cruel to him. For the eighteen years she'd lived blissfully oblivious to the damage it did to Edward and to so many others.

It was part of why she'd left England. Not just to get away from the pain of being jilted, but to escape the system of hierarchies and discrimination. She'd imagined America would be better.

It wasn't.

And here she was, ten years later, heart still aching.

She felt so damn powerless.

But there was a man across the room. Mere feet from her. And she was not powerless when it came to him.

Later, she'd demand the details of what he had not told her about Alfred. Tomorrow. In the light of the morning.

But this night belonged to them alone, and she did not want to spend it arguing.

She stood, crossing the space between them slowly. Step by deliberate step, so that there would be no misunderstanding between them.

When she reached the table, she set one hand flat upon the surface. Then she lowered herself into his lap.

He did not speak as she reached down and cupped his face, one hand on either side, and tipped it up. No protest that this was madness, that it would end in disaster and heartbreak. Those things were all probably true. But they were alone, they were trapped in this room. And it felt like a gift she'd be foolish to throw away.

Yet Edward's eyes were still glazed—and not with the lust that had lit within her the second she sat down in his lap.

That was a lie. It had been burning from the moment she'd seen his face in that ballroom days ago. Maybe it had never gone out entirely, just burned inside of her, a secret ember. A piece of her soul that belonged solely to him.

"What is it?" she asked softly, the words thought barely given form in the softest of whispers.

Edward's eyes closed, as if he couldn't bear to look at her. Panic flooded her chest, but she did not flinch. She waited with all the patience of a decade.

Finally, the lids lifted and those dark eyes found hers.

"I shouldn't have... I... I am sorry you had to see all of that. I never want..." He paused, trying to master himself. Persephone could see the effort etched in his features. "I never wanted you to see that side of me. But I would rather kill a hundred men, die myself, than let them hurt you."

She crashed her mouth against his. Waiting a second, waiting for him to finish his thought, was far, far too long. She'd wasted precious days without her mouth on his and now that she had him, she did not know if she would ever be able to stop.

Chapter Fifteen

Precious seconds.

She could have counted them on one hand.

That was all she had before Edward took control—until she happily surrendered herself to the dominance of his tongue sliding into her mouth, his hands bracketing her hips. When she kissed Edward, her mind stopped. There were no swirling possibilities, no chains of action and reaction to consider.

All of it narrowed to him. The scrape of his teeth over her lower lip, that one slightly jagged tooth from where he'd fallen and chipped it as a child snagging and causing a delicious pinprick of pain. The way his hands, calloused from years of sailing and working alongside his employees, dragged over the fabric of her gown. She could only imagine how they would feel on her skin.

She did not want to imagine.

She wanted to *know*.

They were a tangle of lips and teeth and touches, trying to fill the void of ten years spent apart, ten years spent wanting.

His lips were on her mouth, but then they were on her throat.

She arched into his touch, knowing his hands would be there to steady her. One hand slid up the column of her spine, massaging just between her shoulder blades, while the other was tight on her waist, holding her in his lap.

"Edward," she gasped as he sucked at her pulse. Not an admonition. A prayer.

His only response was a low moan against her throat, then the slide of his mouth lower, lower, lower.

"Get it off," she ordered as his tongue delved beneath the square neckline of her gown.

"So demanding," he scoffed.

But a few adept moves and her gown was falling away to the floor. Persephone had never thought she'd be thankful to be in the arms of a rake.

He nudged aside her chemise, unlacing her corset, drawing one stiff nipple between his teeth. Suddenly, his arms were not enough to hold her. She grabbed for his shoulders to keep herself from falling. Oblivion she'd take, the hard floor was less appealing.

But her fingers caught on fabric—silk. He still wore his waistcoat, the fine shirt beneath. Oh no, that was entirely unacceptable.

She was not nearly as skilled at removing a lover's clothes. But what she lacked in finesse she more than made up for in determination. Edward did not even flinch at the buttons she ripped free in her haste to get the waistcoat off of him, to peel back the linen and toss it to the floor. Persephone did not even notice the damage she did to his fine clothing. His skin. That was all that mattered. The silky golden planes of it beneath her hands, digging her nails into the thick muscles.

Edward groaned, the hand on her waist shoving her down, grinding against—

Oh, yes. Oh heavens above, yes, yes, yes.

Layers of fabric separated them, but the feel of his hard cock pressing up between her legs was a demand that could not be denied. A rush of wetness and heat at her core came in fast, immediate answer.

"Edward." Her voice was hoarse now, thick with need and words she couldn't even form. She did not have that sort of ability any more. All she could do was feel.

It never even occurred to her to resist as his hands returned to her waist, lifting her. Not for the bed, but the table. He set her right on the edge of it, coming to stand so they were face to face.

Edward pressed his forehead to hers, both damp with perspiration and heat that had nothing to do with the fire smoldering in the hearth. For a long heartbeat, they were frozen, just sharing breath. Another heartbeat. Another.

"Persephone," he murmured against her mouth. A question.

She slid her arms down his shoulders and pressed her lips to his in answer.

The world shifted. She was falling. No, Edward was leaning her back on the table. Easing her down, down, down, until her back was flat against the surface. He lingered for a moment, drawing whorls on her throat with his tongue. Then he was sliding back down her body.

His hand followed his mouth, his palm skating over her undergarments, toying with them so he could get at the skin beneath. But all of it was in passing, short of the real goal. When his knees hit the floor, she understood what that goal was.

Her—splayed across his table like his own personal feast.

Another rush of heat and wetness between her legs.

Legs that he was parting, sliding her undergarments away so he could see every inch of her beneath.

He sucked in a breath and for a fraction of a second unease filled her chest.

Persephone dragged in a breath of her own, forcing herself to rise up onto her elbows so she could see his face.

The awe she saw there nearly knocked her back down.

The words etched in his face, the emotion. She knew what it meant without having to hear them from his lips. She had to force her eyes shut at the intensity of it, falling back, trying to survive the waves of emotion that rolled through her in response.

Edward pressed careful kisses to the insides of her thighs, so exceedingly gentle where her legs had rubbed together. Tenderness for tenderness.

His nose nudged at her curls, his deep inhale the only sound in the entire room. Followed by her gasp as he flicked his tongue over her.

Long, lazy swipes of his tongue. Meant to taste, to tease, to savor.

Persephone found herself gripping the edges of the table, arching her back upward. Her bottom lip was going to start bleeding from the torture she was inflicting upon it.

"There's no one to hear you but me, Xīngān," Edward said, his head still buried between her legs. "Scream as loud as you like."

She did not hold back her moan as he slid his tongue not along her folds, but *inside* of her. Making love to her with his tongue, curving it to caress the sensitive walls of her channel, until she wasn't even sure she was breathing, just moaning again and again. Moaning, not screaming—

He swiped his tongue over her center of ultimate pleasure.

Screaming was a polite way of describing the feral sound that ripped from her chest.

Then he did it again.

"Edward. Oh, Edward. My love, my love." She wasn't going to last much longer. She was not going to *exist* much longer. Surely a body could not go on like this. She'd combust into fire and stars and *pleasure*...

"Let go, Xīngān. I have you," Edward urged. The rush of cold from lifting his mouth away, then the sudden insistent pressure of his tongue flicking back and forth, undid her completely.

She came in his hands, in his mouth, his completely.

She'd always been his.

Her legs were quivering, the force of her climax still shuddering out of her. Edward stroked the tops of her thighs, up and down in a slow and repetitive calming motion. When she was steadier, he leaned forward and took her lips in a sweeping kiss.

Heavens above... she could taste herself on his lips.

That sent a whole new wave of satisfaction through her. She wrapped her tongue around his, desperate for the taste of the two of them mingled together. He let her have it for a moment longer before sweeping her up into his arms.

She didn't need to question—she knew where they were going. The bed. Finally, the bed.

Oh so gently he eased her down onto the narrow bed, then maneuvered his massive body in behind her. It should have been impossible to move such a large, muscular form with such grace. She was determined to rediscover every dip and curve of him.

His arm came around her, she was already turning—

"No."

Persephone's body turned to ice.

But then Edward's hands were there again, stroking down her arm and across her belly. Tweaking her nipple. His mouth pressed into the curve of her neck as he settled her back against him so that she was fitted perfectly into his chest. His cock was hard as steel, pressing into the soft mounds of her bottom. She reached for him, but again he caught her hand.

"Persephone," he groaned softly.

She whimpered against him. "Let me—"

"Let me hold you, Xīngān."

The resistance winked away. The entreaty in his voice, the undisguised need in each of those syllables... it had nothing to do with lust.

Her answer did not come in words.

She curled even tighter against him, her own hand closing

around his forearm where it pressed into her chest. She pressed a line of gentle, lingering kisses along the bare, muscled arm. Edward nuzzled into her hair, breathing her in.

As her eyes drifted closed, Persephone exhaled. For the first time since returning from New York, she'd finally come home.

Chapter Sixteen

Sometime in the night, he woke to the feeling of Persephone's hand curled around his cock. And while the lucid Edward, the one who cared about consequences and the future, had protested that it was enough, that he needed nothing more than to hold her... that Edward was still asleep.

But the primal, needy one was not.

This Edward thrust into her hand, savoring the feel of her fingers tight around the base of his cock. He didn't complain when she cupped his balls, rolling them across her palm, squeezing each one with just enough pressure to send his head rolling back, a deep moan vibrating from inside his chest.

It was not any widow or wanton woman looking for an affair who held his cock. It was not a warm body he'd paid to be there. It was Persephone pressed against him, heavy breasts pillowing out against his chest. Persephone, who gave and gave and gave to him. Who loved him, even when it was so damn dangerous for her to do so. He knew she loved him—ten years ago, now, it all blurred together. What mattered was that she was his. He was hers.

Persephone. Persephone. Persephone.

Her name was a chant in his mind, his heartbeat, the thrum of the very blood in his veins.

He belonged to her. He'd always belonged to her. Heart, body, and soul.

Of course, she should touch him like this. His body was hers to use as she wanted.

If she stopped, rolled away, left him near completion and frustrated, that was her choice. If she framed her knees on either side of his hips and took him deep inside of her, he would not protest.

Anything she wanted.

Anything for his Persephone. His goddess. His reason for breathing.

He was so close to climaxing, the steady, insistent pressure of her hand bringing him dangerously near the edge. .

He opened his mouth to warn her before he spilled himself, but before he could get the words out she sealed his mouth in a kiss. A hot, searing plunge of her tongue into the recesses of his mouth.

Then she was gone. Her mouth was gone, but she held still his cock.

Her mouth was sliding across his chin and down his throat. Along his chest. Past where she'd unfastened his trousers until—

Edward jerked back in the bed, grabbing for the wall, the bedsheets, anything to anchor himself to reality as Persephone swiped her tongue over the head of his cock. He felt the seeds of his unrestrained desire, one after another beading on the tip, only to be licked greedily away.

One hand slid down the bedsheets to tangle in her mass of silky curls. He tried with all his might to hold himself back, not to force her head down over him.

But it did not matter, because Persephone was doing it herself. She took him fully into her mouth, past where it should have been possible, into her throat until the tip of his cock nudged at the soft skin of her palate.

One more warning.

"Persephone," he choked out, "I am going to—"

The last words disappeared into a throaty bellow as Persephone's hands closed around his balls once again.

Edward poured himself inside of her, unable to hold himself back. He tried to pull away, to give her an out, but she did not want or need it. She held him in her mouth, letting him jerk inside of her, rolling her tongue lovingly around the side of his cock as he spent himself entirely.

He had no words. He pulled her up his body, his hands already traveling down, seeking her center to return the pleasure she'd given him. But she was kissing his throat, nibbling at his pulse. She arrived back at his mouth.

In the tiny amount of moonlight that leaked in from the curtain she'd left ajar, he watched as she licked that last of his wetness off of her lower lip and gave him a feline smile.

Even as his breath shuddered out of him, she was burrowing down into his shoulder, pulling the blanket up around them. He tried to slide his hand between them, but Persephone hooked her leg around his and pushed herself against him so fully there wasn't even a fraction of an inch of space.

A few seconds later, her breathing evened out. Asleep again.

But Edward laid awake.

Minutes, hours.

He was afraid to close his eyes, for fear he would wake and find himself in a reality where none of this could ever happen again.

Chapter Seventeen

Persephone woke to the sound of gulls and the bright sort of sunshine that only exists in the deep of winter, when the frost and snow reflect back the morning rays and light the world.

She was already hanging half off the bed. The only thing keeping her from the floor was Edward's arm, cuffed snuggly around her waist. As she was contemplating how she'd extricate herself—she had a pressing need for the chamber pot—he let out a soft snore and rolled to his back. She seized her opportunity, sliding free of the bed in a move that was anything but graceful. But there was no audience to judge.

No one to notice how long she stood there, her nightclothes disheveled from the night before, and just looked at him.

Her eyes traced the long line of his legs in his black trousers, still hanging onto his hips. His bare chest rose and fell with each steady, slumbering breath as she admired the flat stomach, broad chest, chiseled muscles.

The same man she'd fallen in love with ten years ago... and yet not. He was sharper now, his muscles tighter. All the youthful softness was gone, and in its wake was only devastating, unyielding perfection.

Even the blanket they'd shared did not dare to cover him from her view, pooled beside him now. He'd wake soon, she knew. The chill in the room, the fire burned down to sad little embers, would wake him without the warmth of her body and the thick woolen blanket. That chill finally permeated the layer of heat that had insulated her since rising, as did the reminder of her body.

Persephone saw to her needs as quietly as she could, then drifted toward the wall of windows. She'd thought she'd closed them tightly after peering out the night before, but apparently not.

She'd been more than a little distracted.

It was the parted curtain that allowed the bright sunshine in. She was grateful for her mistake as she let it caress her skin through the glass.

Moving as soundlessly as she could, she unlatched the window and pressed it open a few inches.

A thin layer of fresh snow coated the rooftops. Down on the street, the thick mud had frozen into a hard crust, topped with a layer of crystalline snow that she knew would not last the hour. Once feet and hooves began to move over it, it would descend into muck once again.

But for that moment, as she dragged in a breath of cold, briny air, and existed above the world where no one could see her or harm her, her skin still warm from Edward's embrace... in that brief moment, everything was perfect.

Then someone began pounding on the warehouse door.

Edward shot to his feet so fast, Persephone questioned what she saw. By the time she blinked, he was already at the window. Not the one where she stood, now shivering and trying not to be terrified, but at the other end of the room. He shoved the curtain aside just enough to peer down.

Whatever he saw... his posture relaxed immediately.

"Stay here," he said, swiping up his shirt from the floor as he passed the table.

He did not pause to lock the apartment door behind him and he left the dagger he'd taken off of their attackers the night before sitting on the table. That was indication enough for her.

She grabbed her cloak off the peg beside the fireplace, threw it around her shoulders, and started down after him. If he'd decided it was not dangerous, then there was no reason for her not to find out what the disturbance was all about. And despite the night spent in each other's arms, he had not been fully honest with her about Alfred's disappearance. An argument they would have this morning, no doubt.

In the meantime, she did not intend to let him shut her out of any new developments.

The pounding continued, mixing with the thump of Edward's bare feet on the stairs. Persephone grabbed the rail, trailing behind him. He was still moving with that fantastical speed.

He yanked the door open without an ounce of hesitation.

Persephone continued after him, her thighs still sore and raw from the night before. She held tight to the rail, but she stumbled. Then her foot caught and she was tumbling.

Edward was a solid wall of muscle at the foot of the stairs.

Her hands splayed across his shoulder blades, her knees buckling and hitting the backs of his thighs. He did not move an inch.

But if he'd hoped that would be enough to hide her from the notice of the woman in the doorway, speaking in rapid Chinese, he was sorely mistaken.

"You have company!" a sharp voice said, switching to English.

Persephone managed to right herself, and though her breathing was coming fast and hard, she had a somewhat-dignified smile in place as she stepped around Edward's shoulder to greet the woman.

Edward promptly shoved her back behind him.

"Do not tell my mother," he barked.

Unable to see over his shoulder, Persephone did hear the other woman's offended gasp. "I would never."

Edward snorted in disbelief, switching back to Chinese.

Persephone would not be shoved about. She retreated a few steps higher, so she could see over Edward's shoulder.

The woman was short and plump, with a round face and arching black eyebrows. As she spoke, she shoved a wrapped parcel into Edward's hands. A second later, the aroma hit Persephone. Meaty, decadent, and best of all, there was steam wafting from the package. Warm.

Edward was nodding and bowing at the waist. Persephone did not need to speak the language to recognize that he was thanking the woman.

"It is no trouble!" the woman said, patting Edward's arm.

Persephone bit her lip to keep in the chuckle. Seeing him at ease was so disarming. And alluring.

That easy smile, the rapid strings of Chinese that rolled so effortlessly from his gloriously talented tongue. Persephone knew a few words, but not nearly enough to follow their conversation. But she was satisfied to watch and listen, to bask in the small, casual moment.

The woman, however, was not. She kept glancing over Edward's shoulder at Persephone. She pulled the cloak a little tighter, hoping that she hadn't revealed what remained of her undergarments in her graceless tumble after Edward.

Persephone ducked her head as her cheeks began to burn, turning to escape back up the stairs.

"I was making another delivery and saw the curtain ajar. I knew if you were here, you'd be wanting your bao."

Edward stilled.

If the woman had spoken a second later, Persephone would have been too far away to notice the snap of tension in Edward.

But luck, it appeared, was on her side that morning. She paused a few stairs above the pair.

"Where else are you delivering bao outside of Limehouse?" Edward asked.

Persephone schooled her face, willing it to show nothing more than polite interest. But the tilt and timbre of Edward's voice had her holding her breath.

The woman's smile faltered. "A woman up at the boarding house two streets over has been special ordering them for a few weeks now."

Persephone squeaked.

Limehouse was the residential district along the Thames where Edward's parents lived, in a small but vibrant Chinese immigrant community. But a boarding house two streets over from where they currently stood was decidedly not in Limehouse. If someone in residence at the boarding house was specially ordering traditional Chinese breakfast...

Edward shot her a brief look over his shoulder that told her not to mention any of the thoughts running rampant through her mind.

Now the woman was *definitely* staring at Persephone.

"Is there something amiss?" she asked, slowly looking back to Edward.

His hand flexed at his side. Then he gave up trying to restrain it and scrubbed his palm over his eyes instead. "So many things I cannot even list them at the moment, Mrs. Tso," he sighed.

The woman's dark eyes went round with interest, but before she could speak Edward cut her off with a sharp bark.

"Do not mention any of this to my mother."

Chapter Eighteen

"**S**he knows your mother?" Persephone asked as soon as the warehouse door locked behind Mrs. Tso.

He scrubbed a hand over his face for the second time that morning. A vulnerability he granted almost no one. And now he'd done it twice.

"Of course, she does," he sighed as he waved Persephone up the stairs. Following her was sweet torture, her wide bottom swaying from side to side. He tried to focus higher up, on her mess of dark hair. But then he remembered how those curls felt tangled around his fingers. He gripped the railing tightly enough to see the whites of his knuckles even in the dim warehouse.

"There are not many Chinese women in London," he said. "Mostly it's men who come off the ships and decide to settle here, marry Englishwomen. The women who are here—"

"Are a tightly knit community?" Persephone finished as she entered the apartment and shrugged off the cloak.

Leaving her in nothing but her undergarments. One breast practically hanging out. Her lips were still swollen from his hungry kisses the night before.

Holy rutting hell.

"A gossip-hungry one," he said hoarsely as the full impact of the woman before him—and the ramifications of Ms. Tso seeing her there—hit him with the force of a hammer.

"She will tell your mother that I was here." Her color began to rise, pink coating her ample bosom and neck before spreading across her cheeks. But she spoke steadily. "We have been seen publicly together. It is possible your mother will have already heard."

Edward sighed, sitting down in the chair still askew from the night before and pulling on his boots. "A fact of which I am painfully aware."

Persephone did not move to straighten what little clothing she wore, nor to reach for the other layers. "What will your mother say?"

"She will be overjoyed," he said with complete honesty. Eugenia Johns had adored Persephone when they'd first met ten years ago. Approved their engagement wholeheartedly. And had not-so-subtly berated him when he'd broken things off. Not to mention the grief she'd given him over the past decade for his insistence on brothels and widows over wedding bells. "And then I will have to disappoint her later."

Disappoint her. Because this arrangement between him and Persephone was temporary. Edward had imagined that he could make it permanent. That he would win her back and they could have a real future together now that he was more accepted by the *ton*.

But he had been fooling himself.

That was the thought that had kept him awake long into the night, when he should have been drifting into a sated sleep from Persephone's attentions.

His status among the *ton* may have changed over the last ten years.

But the rest of the world had not.

Those villains in the alley had not cared about his wealth or his station. They only saw his face. That alone was enough to put Persephone in danger.

And that was utterly unacceptable.

Persephone was staring at him, wringing her hands as all his hopes for the future fell down around him. She misunderstood the expression on his face.

"I would never want to cause your mother pain," she said with a heavy sigh.

Edward had not considered his family's reaction to Persephone. The fact that his mother had not hunted him down in the last week spoke to her isolation in Limehouse. But now that Mrs. Tso had seen Persephone, there would be no way to avoid his mother.

None of it was Persephone's fault. That squarely rested with him. He'd devised this scheme in order to stay close to her. Selfishly thinking he could have her. He would hurt her again. He wanted to fall to his knees and beg her forgiveness for the pain. Tell her he loved her. Let her hold his head tight against her breasts as he cursed the world.

But he did not do any of that.

Instead, he said, "That is not your concern."

Her eyes flashed with hurt.

It was not her concern, because *he* was not her concern.

As much as he wanted to sweep her up in his arms and take her back to bed, that was daylight shining through the curtains. They could not pretend that last night had been anything other than madness. It could not be a herald of some happily ever after. That sort of ending did not exist for them, and he had to accept it.

When he stood up, reaching for his waistcoat, Persephone had straightened her undergarments. Her dark eyes were masked, no hurt visible.

Good girl.

He held out her gown.

She accepted it and began dressing with quick, efficient movements. "Why did you ask her about the boarding house?"

"I would have thought you'd already worked that out." He finished the last button on his tailcoat.

She was standing with her back to him, the delicate column of her spine—

"I need you to button my gown." Her voice was frostier than the rooftops outside.

Edward painstakingly fastened each button without brushing his fingertips against her skin.

"Kidnappers do not order their prisoner's breakfast of choice," Persephone said, waiting for him to tell her that he'd finished. She did not know he'd finished moments before, that he was savoring the unseen seconds to breathe her in before they were parted forever.

She turned her head to check his progress and he was forced to step back.

"True," he agreed. "But I do not know of any other Chinese residents within ten blocks of this warehouse. And as I said—"

"They all know each other," she finished for him. She met his gaze, her dark eyes steady—the emotions of the night before firmly locked away.

"What aren't you telling me about Alfred's disappearance?" The quiet, resolute command in her voice was impossible to miss.

He could not tell her the truth. At least, not the whole truth. That he'd led her to believe the situation direr than it actually was so that he might have more time with her. That he'd seized upon her hopes for a husband and a family to get her to agree to a fake courtship, so he might have a chance of showing her that he loved her still. She did not deserve all of that extra pain.

He sucked in a breath and curled his fist at his side to keep from rubbing it over his face again. "Alfred has gotten him into scrapes like this before."

Persephone's dark brown eyes widened. "He has been kidnapped before?" she cried.

"No, this is a new scenario," Edward admitted. "But he has disappeared without explanation before. Hidden to avoid gambling debts or taking on any sort of responsibility at the company."

He watched as her delicate hands curled into fists. If she took a swing at him, he would not stop her. He more than deserved it.

"He is not in any danger," she said, lower lip wobbling.

Edward suppressed his cringe. "Very doubtful."

She shook her head, dark curls flying. "Why, Edward? Why insist on my help if it was not urgent to begin with?'

Because I love you.

Because I think you still love me, too.

He had no excuse. Maybe that was why he said, "It was a mistake." Then a heartbeat later. "I am sorry."

And he was. Sorry he'd hurt her ten years ago. Sorry that he'd been naïve enough to think they could have a future now. Sorry that he'd dragged her into this mess and could not come up with a way to spare her feelings.

He expected vitriol. He certainly deserved it.

But instead, Persephone's mouth softened. She did not excuse or forgive him. But she dipped her chin, just an inch, in acknowledgement of his words.

Edward fisted his hands at his side as well to resist the urge to twine the dark curl trailing over her shoulder around his finger and pull her close. "What are the odds that once you're dressed, you will let me put you in a hackney back to Mayfair?"

"Nonexistent."

"As I thought."

He sighed and sat back down at the table, opening the parcel Mrs. Tso had left. At least they had breakfast.

* * *

"These streets do not look nearly as intimidating as they did in the dark," Persephone mused as they walked through the midmorning light.

"You won't feel that way if we come across our friends from last night," Edward said. From the corner of his eye, he watched her shiver slightly. But he did not reach for her or try to tuck her arm into his. The warmth of the night had cooled into a brittle iciness.

It was for the best.

Persephone bit her lower lip, eyes scanning each person they passed. "I expect you'd put them down as easily as you did before."

The heat in her voice was unmistakable.

His cock surged in response.

That ice, it seemed, was only a thin layer. Beneath it, they were both still churning with heat.

They carefully avoided talking—and looking at each other—for the rest of the walk to the boarding house two streets away.

"Here it is." Edward stopped in front of the old but tidy building. He must have walked by it a hundred times or more over the past several years. It was one of the more well-maintained boarding houses on the dockside. Not the type he referred his sailors to. He turned to Persephone to hear the plan she undoubtedly had bubbling in her mind.

She was already up the steps, pounding on the door.

"Persephone—"

"Hello! My husband and I have just arrived from Portsmouth and would like to inquire about a room for the week."

Edward struggled to determine who was more poleaxed—him, or the straight-backed woman standing in the doorway with a dirty apron, a neat dark blue gown, and flour on her hands.

Persephone's bright smile did not budge an inch as the woman, the landlady, looked them both over.

Persephone had left off her cloak, despite the brisk morning air, leaving her fine wool pelisse on full display. The steel-haired woman looked her up and down, noting the intricate pattern of leaves embroidered around the collar and the inlaid tortoiseshell buttons.

"I am Mrs. Pickering. My husband and I run the boarding-house. We may have an accommodation that would suit."

"Lovely!" Persephone preened, threading her arm through Edward's as Mrs. Pickering led them inside.

A squeeze of her hand on his arm—telling him to keep his mouth shut as they were shown into a shabby but impeccably clean sitting room at the front of the house, overlooking the street. There were fresh scones, coffee, and tea on the sideboard.

Yes, much too nice of an establishment for his sailors.

He listened silently as Persephone spoke with the landlady, discussing the two rooms she had available. Persephone listed details of their fake life together with startling ease.

My husband is a clerk for Johns Maritime Enterprises and we're looking for a permanent residence in London. Yes, the room sounds lovely, but we do have our children to consider. My family is abroad just now, but being close to them will be such a joy.

It was almost as if she was reciting a fantasy. Her fantasy.

Before the implications of that could fully register, Mrs. Pickering led them up a narrow set of stairs to the first floor.

"We have another of your husband's countrymen in residence," the matron was saying as she gained the landing.

They already knew that.

But a thrill of anticipation stuttered to life in his stomach.

Persephone made a show of looking around the room before declaring it perfectly suited for their stay.

"I require three nights' fee up front," Mrs. Pickering said, making no move to leave.

Both women slid their eyes to Edward.

Only when she'd been paid did she hand them a key from the massive ring tucked into the pockets of her dress. And only when she'd disappeared down the staircase, back through the sitting room towards the kitchen at the rear of the house, did Persephone start knocking on doors.

"What are you doing?" Edward demanded. But the door was already swinging open to reveal a staid, middle-aged woman who very decidedly did not look like she wanted to meet her new neighbors.

Persephone was not the type to be deterred by a mere glare.

"Hello, we've just taken the room down the hall. How lovely to meet you and your...?" She stood on her tiptoes to look past the woman into the room. Edward nearly expired on the spot.

"It is just me," the woman said, eyes narrowing as she sighted him over Persephone's shoulder.

"Lovely!" Persephone cried.

She cringed as the door closed in her face.

Edward crossed his arms over his body. "Is that how the Lady Fixer did things in New York?"

"Sometimes a blunt approach is what's needed. Unless you'd rather we waste time on a lead that does not, in fact, help us find your brother."

Edward begrudgingly uncrossed his arms. She pointed across the landing. "Start knocking."

They had no luck at either of the doors on the first floor. Both were locked, but neither occupant was answering their knocks. Edward could pick a simple lock, but with Mrs. Pickering below...

"Go knock on the doors upstairs. I will remain here, in case any of the occupants of these two rooms," she pointed between the two unopened doors, "Try to sneak away."

Edward sighed—of course, she had a plan. Of course, it was terrible.

"And what will you do if the kidnappers try to smuggle Alfred out through one of these doors?"

She pulled her penknife out of her boot. He'd wiped it clean, but there was still a glimmer of blood at the base. "I shall scream very loud and then stab them," she declared. A threat made much less intimidating by the fact that he'd disclosed his lack of concern for the kidnappers' true nefariousness.

He almost insisted that she come with him. But the longer he spent in this decorous, tidy boarding house, the more he doubted that anything untoward would happen with Mrs. Pickering on guard. Not the place to find a kidnapped hostage—not the place they would find Alfred.

But he'd already paid for three days in a room he had no intention of occupying. He may as well check the upper two rooms.

He left Persephone humming to herself. She had either entirely recovered from their encounter with the villains and the subsequent... activities. Or she was putting up a wall so thick, not even he could break through it.

He could hardly blame her.

The second floor was smaller than the first. One door was unlocked—the second unoccupied room that Mrs. Pickering would have offered them if Persephone had not exclaimed so effusively over the larger, more expensive one.

He lifted his hand to the second door and knocked, mind already turning to the next path. Persephone would be forming her own plan right now as he waited for a response.

A thump from the other side of the door.

Edward drew the knife he'd taken from their attackers.

Footsteps—light, careful, to sneak up on him.

He took two steps back, ready to ram the door with his shoulder and break it down.

But the door swung open. No villain sprung out to face him. The footsteps—not a man sneaking. A woman.

A beautiful young woman whose face he knew, crowned with golden hair.

And over her shoulder, laying on the bed, chewing on a hearty bite of bao, was his younger brother.

Chapter Nineteen

The color drained from the courtesan's face. She staggered back, the surprise of his arrival as good as a physical blow.

Edward knew the second his brother sighted him. He sat straight up in the bed, the bun falling from his hand as he stared in open-mouthed disbelief.

Alfred scrambled to his feet. "Edward—"

"*No.*"

He held out one hand. The entire scene froze. Madeline quaking at the door, Alfred half-clothed, half-off the bed, bao abandoned on the rug.

Edward took one step back on the landing and called down the stairs. "Persephone, come up here."

Alfred jerked into motion. "Persephone? *Your* Persephone?"

"You do not get to ask questions," Edward ordered, tracking his brother out of the corner of his eye. There was one window. But he doubted even his brother was stupid enough to try and escape out of it now.

Persephone's voice preceded her as she climbed the stairs. "Nothing untoward down here. Though the woman who answered the first door did open it, see me standing there, and shut—" Her mouth hung open in utter shock. Edward caught her arm, in case she swooned. But she shook him off, walking right past him into the room and straight up to Alfred, as if his brother was an apparition who might vanish at any moment. "Alfred."

"Hullo, Persephone." Alfred scratched at his hair, still mussed from bed. "You look well."

"You look..." She paused long enough take in his appearance and to note the young woman at the door. "You do not look like someone who was kidnapped and held for ransom."

"That is because he was not," Edward said sharply, glaring at his brother. "Unless I failed so miserably in teaching you fisticuffs that even a tiny harlot can restrain you against your will."

"I think any restraining was entirely at his will," Persephone said, glancing between Alfred's shirtless form and the courtesan in her dressing gown.

Edward rolled his eyes. "Get dressed." He jerked his chin between the room's two original occupants. "It would be undignified for me to murder you in your undergarments."

He tugged Persephone back out onto the landing. Only once the door was closed again did he let out a shuddering sigh.

Persephone's eyes were intent—not on the door that had just closed, but on him. "What does this mean?"

"That Alfred is a bigger fool than I ever thought." His mind was sifting through possibilities, searching for any explanation that did not involve his brother being an absolute arse. But each scenario that would have absolved him was as unlikely as the next.

A headache began to thump at the base of his skull.

How did Persephone survive with her brain constantly in motion like this?

"He really staged the entire thing?" She pulled out the ransom note, tucked into the pocket of her pelisse. Edward did not remember how or when she'd gotten possession of it again.

This time, he did not bother trying to take it back from her. "He will either tell us the truth or I will beat it out of him."

She caught her lower lip between her teeth. "He is still your brother."

"I will take your concern under advisement."

"No you won't."

The door swung open once again, revealing Alfred in trousers and a shirt, a vest hastily buttoned over the top. Madeline, for her part, had put on a day gown and corralled her blonde mane into a presentable knot atop her head. He supposed life in a brothel called for making oneself presentable at a moment's notice.

"Please, come in," Alfred said.

As if he were inviting them into the parlor for tea. Edward tensed, but Persephone's hand closed around his arm. She stayed close at his side as they entered.

An offer of silent support. Or an attempt to tamp down his temper.

He was not going to question it just then. Not when he was far too busy questioning *everything else*.

One glance around the room and it was obvious. There was an armoire in the corner, the door ajar enough to reveal the neatly folded clothing within. An open trunk stood beside it, the contents decidedly frillier and more feminine. Books, a chess set, a half-drunk bottle of wine.

"You've been here all along."

Alfred cringed. "Edward, let me explain—"

"I knew you were a wastrel. But *this* is how determined you are to shirk your responsibilities? Faking a kidnapping, causing me worry, extorting your own brother for money?" He flung out a hand in Madeline's direction. "Unless you are somehow about to convince me that she kidnapped you."

"None of this is her fault," Alfred said, stepping in front of Madeline.

"Given the state in which I found you two, I doubt that."

"Surely you are not going to place the blame upon a powerless woman and absolve your brother," Persephone cried, swatting his arm.

He resisted the urge to swat her right back.

"I am doing no such thing. But she lied to me in that brothel," he said through his teeth. Understanding flashed in Persephone's eyes. "And he certainly knew about it."

Persephone's eyes swept back over the couple, with a sharper edge this time. "They are both complicit."

"Are you going to allow me to speak?" Alfred asked. He had the audacity to cross his arms over his chest and look as if he was the one put out by the whole situation.

Edward was going to lose his mind. Maybe it was already gone. Maybe he was still asleep in the warehouse and this ridiculous sequence of events was all a strange after effect of his night with Persephone.

"Edward, perhaps we should hear what he has to say before issuing any blame at all? Perhaps there is a perfectly reasonable explanation for this... unusual behavior." She was grappling, and they both knew it. Alfred did too, from the way he avoided Persephone's eyes.

Enough of this. He needed to speak with his brother, man to man.

"Persephone, will you please go fetch us something to drink?"

Her eyebrows nearly disappeared into her dark hairline. The hand on the arm she did not hold curled into a fist, bracing for an argument.

Persephone raked her gaze over him, all sharp judgment and annoyance. But whatever she saw there—whatever he revealed without meaning to—her eyes softened, just a fraction. When they landed back on Alfred, the softness was gone.

"I will go and see about a nip of brandy or whisky. I am certain Mrs. Pickering will have just the thing to steady our nerves," she said, though she was obviously not pleased to do it. She wanted answers nearly as badly as he did.

She was halfway out the door when Edward added, "Take Madeline with you."

Edward did not miss the subtle nod his brother sent the other woman.

"Mabel, actually," the blonde woman said as she stepped onto the landing with Persephone.

"Bloody hell," Edward cursed under his breath.

He waited until Persephone's cheery voice was too far away to hear before rounding on his brother.

"You better have a damned-good explanation for all of this."

Alfred retreated a step, then another. Until he was standing at the foot of the four-poster bed, clutching one of the foot posts.

Edward stepped further into the room. "Do you want me to start guessing?"

Alfred wrinkled his nose, but he did speak.

"A friend got their sister to write the ransom note," he began. "She thought it was a jape."

"Elizabeth Bradshaw."

Alfred's eyes widened. "How did—"

"Persephone has become quite resourceful over the years." Edward sighed, shaking his head. He still could not make sense of it. The sequence of events was clear enough to comprehend, but the motivation... "Why have the note written at all? Why do any of this? I knew you were up to something, that you'd gotten yourself into some sort of stupid mess. But faking your own kidnapping? What reason could you possibly have for this?"

He could hear Persephone's words, echoing in his head. *Hear what he has to say...*

Alfred stared. Maybe he hoped that Edward would keep ranting, that he'd avoid having to account for his actions.

Edward would not allow it. He let the silence stretch, let it press in on them, until Alfred's knuckles shone moon-white around the bedpost and his brow was wrinkled in self-induced agony.

"I apologize for any worry I caused. I figured you would not take it too seriously, given my history," he said.

"The ransom note promised bodily harm in no uncertain terms if the ransom was not paid in full." Edward was not interested in coddling his younger brother. Even if he'd never believed Alfred in any imminent danger.

He knew Alfred had been unhappy for several months, but this... it ought to have been unfathomable.

Alfred cringed. "I know, I—"

Footsteps pounded up the stairs. Persephone appeared, her dark eyes wide, Madeline nowhere in sight.

"I am so sorry," Persephone whispered, clutching his arm. But she only used it to lever herself away, around the door to reveal—

"Alfred Hàoyú Johns! How dare you get yourself kidnapped!" their mother shrieked.

Chapter Twenty

E dward had thought the situation could not get worse.

But he was so, so, very wrong.

As Eugenia Johns looked from one son to the other, she wore the exact same expression she had when he was a boy—right before she removed her shoe and smacked him with it. He doubted that twenty years, or Persephone's presence, would prevent her from doing just that, just then.

To Edward's eternal and undying relief, Richard Johns appeared in the doorway of the room a second later.

His father surveyed the scene with the efficiency Edward had come to expect over a lifetime. Sailor, sea captain, shipping magnate. Richard Johns had handled much more delicate and dangerous situations. But Edward did not miss the slight flinch in his father's blue eyes as they skittered over his mother.

"I expect to find one son, but instead I've found two," his father said, that deep, booming voice filling the small room. But his eyes softened when they landed on Persephone. "And then some."

"It is a pleasure to see you, Mr. Johns," Persephone said, dropping into a graceful curtsey. She offered the same—and a smile—to his mother. "Mrs. Johns."

His mother's face transformed immediately, the hard line of her mouth melting as she brushed past Edward to clasp Persephone's hand affectionately. "Oh darling, you know you must always call me Eugenia."

Edward did not know whether to be thankful or suspicious of that warm welcome. "Mā—"

"Oh no—I do not want to hear from either of you. One son receives a ransom note promising imminent injury to his younger brother and does not tell me about it, and the other orchestrates a pretend kidnapping in order to..." she broke off in a string of Chinese so rapid, it was nearly unintelligible even to Edward. He did not even have time to dart his gaze to Persephone, to ask how his mother knew about the note he'd received.

He opened his mouth to protest, but the room erupted.

"Have you lost your—"

"—Persephone should not be—"

"Who is the young woman downstairs?"

"Bà, please—"

"Do not appeal to your father!"

Richard grabbed his wife's hand just short of jabbing her younger son in sharply in the chest. With her hand firmly enclosed in his, he turned back to Edward and Persephone.

"Persephone, I am so sorry that you have been caught up in this little family squabble," he said.

Edward had not realized that he'd moved in front of Persephone, unconsciously shielding her from the chaos. Not that she had anything to fear from his family. But the instinct to protect was so strong, he could not stop himself.

"I am merely glad to find that Alfred is safe," she said slowly, moving so she stood beside Edward rather than behind him.

"Indeed. Aren't we all?" Eugenia rounded back on her

younger son. "You have one minute to explain yourself, or I will—"

"Eugenia," Richard said, easing her back.

The headache that had started to throb on the landing had graduated to fully-fledged pounding. Edward loved his family, but when they were all together like this... he preferred the chaos of a ship in a storm.

And when they were arguing... it made the altercation in the alleyway the night before appear docile.

His father looked between his two sons with the steely, demanding gaze that had cowed many a sailor and investor over the last three decades.

But it was Edward he addressed, rather than the son who'd sunk down to sit on the edge of the bed. "Why didn't you come to me about the ransom note?"

Guilt rose up in his stomach, clawing at his chest. But before it could fully take hold, a hand brushed against his. *Persephone.*

The softest touch—of solidarity and support.

Edward lifted his chin.

"I wished to protect you from his stupidity," he said, ignoring Alfred's offended grunt at his choice of words and focusing wholly on their father instead. "You received a note as well?" They must have, to know he'd been kidnapped.

His father nodded. "We kept it from you for the same reason."

His mother was not so patient. She threw up her free hand in frustration. "Enough of this. Alfred, explain yourself."

Alfred's swallow was audible. "I did not mean for any of this to happen."

There it was again—the brush of Persephone's fingers against his. This time, Edward let his loosen, let her gently interlace them.

"What did you mean to happen, precisely?" he asked his brother.

Alfred stared at his hands. "I wanted the money. That was it

—enough money that I could..." A long, shaking breath. Then his spine straightened, and he looked up to meet their gazes. "That I could take Mabel away. Away from London and away from Johns Maritime Enterprises."

"And Mabel is...?" Eugenia asked, tilting her head. Alfred was taller than her, even sitting. But she looked down her nose at him just the same.

"The young woman waiting in the parlor," Persephone offered. "I think I ought to go keep her company."

His mother's sharp eyes—the twins to his own—turned on Persephone. Edward would have laughed at the way she grabbed his fingers, so tightly, if it had been any other circumstance.

"Do stay. You are practically a member of the family," Eugenia said, the smile she offered Persephone melting away as she turned back, confident her order would be followed.

Persephone did not move an inch toward the still-open door.

Edward's father sighed. Both sons knew what that meant. Their mother was infamously hot tempered, but their father... when he ran out of patience, they were truly hopeless.

"Out with it, Alfred. Beginning to end. And no one—" Richard pointed around the room. "Interrupt."

Alfred's jaw twitched, but his spine remained straight as he addressed them. "I have wanted out of the shipping business for years."

When no one responded, he continued.

"I've spoken to both of you about it. But you both insisted I would change my mind. Realize my responsibility." He looked between his father and Edward. "The fake kidnapping was a bad idea. But I thought... I thought you might finally have some sympathy for me. Then I could use the money to set Mabel and I up somewhere else—Edinburgh, maybe. Or New York."

It made sense—in the most twisted and unacceptable ways.

How had Edward failed to realize the depth of his brother's unhappiness? He *had* spoken about it with Alfred... several times.

But he assumed it was because Alfred had not yet had the chance to sail, to captain his own ship, to grow to love it as Edward had when he was his age.

The fingers twined with his tightened. Persephone.

Her eyes were on him, not Alfred. She'd looked at his carefully unreadable face, and still discerned his inward struggle.

Edward let his mind go blank. Let himself focus on nothing but the connection between them. The softness of her palms against his calloused hands—*when had she removed her gloves?* — the gentle scrape of her fingernail across his knuckle.

He refocused enough to hear the last of Alfred's explanation.

"I met the Bradshaws playing cards. They agreed to have the ransom notes delivered and to be couriers for the money. They thought it was a fantastic jape."

Which was precisely why Edward abjured the ton. Only young men with that amount of privilege would think something like this a *fantastic jape*. And his own brother. *Hell and damnation.*

Several beats of silence filled the room, all of them waiting for another word from Alfred.

But none came.

It was Edward, shaking his head, still struggling to understand, who broke the silence. "All of this, because you could not tell us that you did not want to work with the company?"

His brother stood up. He did not look at their mother or father. He stared right at Edward—right over his shoulder. At Persephone.

"All of this for Mabel," Alfred said quietly, his gaze finally meeting his brother's.

"I see," Edward said with equal softness.

And blast him, but as Persephone's hand squeezed his... he did. He understood making stupid decisions for the sake of love.

"I beg your pardon, I had no notion..."

As one, they all turned towards the open door.

Where Mrs. Pickering stood on the landing, eyes wide as saucers, one hand closed around the neck of a bottle of brandy. "I don't think I've brought enough glasses."

* * *

Several gulps of brandy later—they'd passed the bottle around in lieu of waiting for glasses—Edward escorted Persephone down to the ground floor of the boarding house.

It had taken considerable maneuvering and reminding Persephone of the ever-ticking clock, but Edward had managed to detangle her from his mother's arms. Mr. Pickering, who'd appeared only at the last moment, had gone down ahead of them to find a hackney to take Persephone back to Mayfair before even her tolerant chaperone became concerned.

Which meant these were the last moments Edward would spend in her presence.

And despite all that Alfred had put him through these last weeks, it was this moment that truly had his stomach turning over.

But when they reached the bottom of the stairs, Persephone untangled her hand from his and walked into the parlor.

Madeline—Mabel, he corrected himself, was perched on the edge of the sofa.

"They are waiting for you," Persephone said gently.

The young woman offered a tumultuous smile and then hurried up the stairs.

And then they were alone.

He wanted to kiss her. To pull her tight and ask her not to leave. To stay with him in this world she'd created for Mrs. Pickering, where they had a whole imaginary life together. A world in which she was not the daughter of a duke, and marriage to him would not mean exposing herself to ridicule at best... physical harm at worst.

But Edward did not allow himself to do any of those things. He did not reach for her. He did not kiss her.

She did not reach for him either.

His heart sank. Maybe he'd been misreading her these last few days. Maybe what had happened the night before had been nothing but an interlude to her. A farewell to their past.

He should be glad. He did not want her to suffer like he was, like she'd suffered before.

The door behind Persephone opened. Mr. Pickering was smiling at them and motioning toward the waiting hackney.

He had to say something. Something before she walked out of his life forever. "I shall—"

"—join me for Lady Soren's soiree tomorrow evening?" Persephone finished, her full lips curving.

Edward blinked, not comprehending. "We've found Alfred."

"Alfred was not the only part of our bargain." She did not quite let herself smile. But there it was, the very thing that had kindled in his own heart days before. Hope.

Hope which had been so thoroughly squashed by the harsh reality of the world.

Maybe he was as much a fool as Alfred, because instead of making up an excuse or begging off, he nodded.

"Tomorrow evening, then," he said as she stepped away.

He wished she'd stay, if only to look at his face. The face he'd practiced for so many years to make hardened, unreadable. But which she could decrypt in a manner of seconds.

He wished she'd stay and tell him how he was feeling.

Because Edward had no chance of making sense of it on his own.

Chapter Twenty-One

"Your Mr. Johns has not yet arrived?"

Persephone managed not to cringe at Henry's question, but only just. Madison had been sending more and more obvious looks towards the foyer over the last ten minutes, but it was her husband who'd finally voiced the question.

She should have asked him to meet her at the Warsham residence, rather than the Soren townhouse.

"Edward will keep his promise," she heard herself say. Her eyes were too busy scanning the crowd for her to see the interaction between the husband and wife beside her.

"Promise—ouch!" Henry cried.

Persephone spared them one glance—to find Henry rubbing his upper arm. Madison had either hit him or pinched him for whatever he'd been about to say.

"I am certain that Mr. Johns will arrive very soon," Madison said, her voice a bit too high-pitched. "You did not see the way he stared at Persephone at the Wheeler's charity auction. He is quite infatuated with her."

Or he'd made a good show of pretending to be.

Persephone nibbled at a canape.

What was real, between her and Edward?

She was very really in love with him.

There was no use in denying that to herself any longer.

But what would she do with that realization?

Nothing.

She could do nothing with it.

Three social outings. That is what Edward had promised her in exchange for her assistance in finding Alfred. The latter had been accomplished. The former... he would not break his promise.

Her heart? Most certainly.

But his word... he'd keep that.

"You promised me a waltz," Madison reminded her husband from the periphery of Persephone's senses. They whispered something else, then drifted away, considering her sufficiently chaperoned given that her supposed suitor was nowhere in sight.

Her back pressed against the wall. She'd never been a wallflower.

But the longer she stood here waiting for Edward, the more the reality of it began to crush down on her.

The soiree was small. She could not have missed his arrival.

She had very intentionally not worn a rose in her coiffure. She wanted new clients, having dealt with Miss Anna Winlock's and Lady St. James's matters. But not tonight. Tonight was about her second aim—securing a husband. Which was why she was so concerned about Edward's arrival, or lack thereof.

The charity auction had not been enough. The gentleman of the *ton* had to see her courting the attention of the most unmarriageable man in London, in order for them to want to find out for themselves just what was so enchanting about her.

Persephone shook her head slightly.

It was convoluted enough to make even her rapid-fire, winding mind confused.

She sighed, easing closer to the window. Despite the snow falling outside, it was hot inside the Soren's townhouse. If she was doomed to be a wallflower, at least she could press her back to the cold panes of glass.

"You are making a very good show of looking like the lost, lonely lover."

His breath slid over her shoulders, down the nape of her neck, making her blush in very indecent places.

"I would not look lost or lonely if you were more punctual," she managed to bite back. It came out as more of a purr.

"You did not specify a time."

He stood at her left shoulder. For all observers, he was merely staring out at the crowd, speaking to her in hushed tones. Perfectly proper.

Of course, no one saw the knuckle that Edward ran down the column of her spine.

"How is Alfred?" she forced herself to ask, even as that knuckle skidded lower over her derriere.

"My mother has decided to give Mabel lessons in Chinese."

Her heart jolted. This time, she recognized jealousy's uncomfortable grip.

But she forced herself to smile. "I am so very happy for them."

"There is much still to be settled. I still have not decided how I'm going to punish Alfred. Boxing his ears seems the mildest of sentences. But Mabel spent an entire afternoon with my mother and did not flee, so I think the likelihood of a happy outcome is substantial." Not a knuckle now, but a flick. Thumb and forefinger together, flicking her—in the curve where her bottom met her thigh, at the base of her spine, the nape of her neck...

"I am so happy for them."

Edward paused. "You've already said that."

"It is true."

Happy. Jealous.

His fingertips grazed the sensitive skin just below her hairline.

Burning.

"Come with me," Edward murmured, his breath hot against the tender skin his fingertips had caressed seconds before.

Persephone wished she was still against the wall, just so she would have something to hold her up. "We need to stay here." She nodded toward the small dance floor, where other couples were already swirling. "We could dance."

The sound of contempt from Edward's throat had her smiling despite herself.

"We will come back," he said, dismissing her preposterous proposal outright.

"How are prospective suitors to notice us together if we are not even in the room?" It was a valid response. The reason she'd reminded him of the fabricated outings was to boost her interest to prospective suitors. It certainly wasn't so she could draw out her time with Edward.

Even if she did have feelings for him.

"They will see us leaving together," Edward said.

She jerked her head up to look at him. "So you'd prefer I be ruined?"

Part of her wanted him to say yes. *Yes, I'd prefer you be ruined, so that I could finally claim you as mine.*

But that was not what he said. "Aren't you already?"

Yes.

No.

Not in the eyes of the *ton*.

But in her own heart... yes, he'd ruined her so very thoroughly.

He cupped her bottom, swiping his thumb over the curve proprietarily, still hidden from view of the crowd.

"I am going to make an appearance in Soren's study, where they are currently passing around a twelve-year Scotch whisky. You are going to go to the ladies' retiring room," he said. "I will meet you at the rear stairwell."

"If we are both missing—"

"It will be just enough to draw interest. Not enough to ruin you."

She turned to look up at him fully for the first time that night, searching his face.

The rake looked back at her. Not the protective brother or the stoic professional. Not even the jaded society outsider. Those black eyes were pure seduction, and they were aimed squarely at her.

She should run in the opposite direction.

Instead, she excused herself to the ladies' retiring room.

* * *

"Where are we going?"

Edward did not look back over his shoulder. Merely tightened his hold on her hand. "You shall see."

"We should not be intruding on the earl's private residence." They'd left the rooms fitted out for the soiree, wound through a darkened sitting room, past a piano, and now she wasn't sure where they were.

Edward's soft chuckle filled the darkness around her. And it was so precious, she almost forgot to glare at him when he said, "The Lady Fixer has never wandered where she ought not?"

Almost.

But a minute later, he opened a set of glass doors.

Her breath caught in her throat.

Built onto the side of the house, the glass panels were coated in frost. Overhead, snow was already accumulating. Eventually, it would slide down the slanted glass roof. But just then, with the snow softly falling on three sides of them, the solid townhouse at their backs... Persephone sighed at the majestic beauty of it.

Then her eyes slid downward, to what grew in that warm, sheltered hothouse.

"It's a rose garden in the middle of winter," she breathed.

Edward lifted one of the loose curls she'd left trailing down her back. "I expected to see one in your hair tonight."

"My focus is on other things this evening." An invitation.

He curled the tendril around his finger. "I wondered where you'd gotten the one you wore that first night."

"Madison's sister, Meera. She and her husband travel extensively, and he built her a hothouse last year after they returned from the West Indies." But she did not want to talk about Madison, or Meera, or anyone.

She did not want to talk at all.

She curled her fingers around his where they caressed her hair. Then down past his wrist. Forearm, bicep. Impossibly muscular shoulder.

She tried to memorize every inch.

And what better way to remember his body than to explore it with her own?

Edward was ready, lifting her off her feet the moment her lips touched his. Or did he touch hers? It hardly mattered. They came together, fitted together, like two halves in a set. It had always been like that between them—a perfect match.

Perfect in the way their bodies spoke to one another, their minds. Perfect if they could just stay alone, without the world pressing in on them.

"We are alone now," he said against her lips.

She had not spoken. But he seemed to know her thoughts all the same. "And what will you do about it?"

He swept one hand underneath her knees and carried her between the roses. What other exotic blooms did the earl keep in his greenhouse? Persephone would never know. Her entire existence had narrowed to the points where Edward's body touched hers.

He lowered her down to a settee, pulling back. She whimpered at the loss, but a second later he was there, his body covering hers, his tailcoat tossed aside.

His tongue slid along her throat, cherishing her sensitive skin. But it was too gentle, too soft.

She wanted more. She wanted the burning length of him buried inside of her.

No idle touches. No soft caresses.

She palmed him through his trousers hard enough that he groaned against her throat. Buttons? She made short work of those. Past the undergarments until his hot length was in her hand once more.

"Persephone, Xīngān," he groaned, pulling back on one arm, his hand planted beside her head.

She said no words. Only reached down, pulling up her skirts and undergarments. Letting him see the raw need—to be taken by him, to belong to him, if only for a few minutes. If only this once.

He slid inside of her, and it was *perfection*.

Every fantasy she'd spun herself over the last ten years, every time she'd touched herself in the dark... this was the moment she'd yearned for.

Edward groaned, then buried his mouth in her throat to mask the sound.

So close.

The party continued, just a few doors away. She could still hear the strings of music. But it only intensified the sensation as Edward's cock stretched her, pushing her further. Ten years ago, they'd been adolescents. Wild, determined, enthralled.

But now, this is what it was to be with a man.

The man.

The one she loved.

The word surged through her as her hips lifted off the settee, pulling him deeper.

Edward's breathing was ragged, his chest shaking against hers.

"Darling," he rasped against her throat. "Darling, I won't last if you keep doing that."

He tried to pull back, but she could not allow it. She linked her hands behind his neck, arching her hips to keep him close. She wanted every bit of him—unrestrained, unleashed, only for her. Let her be the reason he lost that sacred control.

"Persephone," he groaned, his hips rocking harder still.

"My love, my love," she chanted. "Give yourself to me."

She'd meant it as a plea, but it came out as a command.

And Edward surrendered to it without argument.

He poured himself inside of her, hot and thick, until the force of it sent her over the edge as well, and she joined him in glorious oblivion.

Oblivion.

Oblivious.

Yes, she'd happily remain there in oblivion with him, oblivious to the world that was determined to keep them apart.

Oblivion did not seem scary at all, so long as she was with Edward.

Chapter Twenty-Two

He could not linger.
Every second they stole was a scandal in the making.

So why was he still entwined in her arms?

The answer was painfully simple—he loved her.

He'd loved her from the moment she smiled at him in that Portsmouth ballroom a decade ago. Every moment since then had been spent loving her.

That bright smile that came so easily.

The dark eyes that read him when no one else could.

The brilliant mind disguised under layers of propriety.

But the young woman he'd loved ten years ago... that love had been young as well. Naïve. Special in the way that only first loves could be, if the romance novels were to be believed.

This thing between them now? It was bigger, stronger, and even more dangerous. It was the kind of love that would devastate him if he gave himself over to it.

Worse than that, it would destroy her.

It would be small, at first.

Less invitations would come. Then her friends would fall out of touch, though they'd offer benign excuses.

Edward had spent nearly thirty years watching his mother receive that sort of scorn, and much worse. His indomitable mother. She'd never once broken under the strain. But in these last few years, she'd rarely left Limehouse without his father.

He did not need to ask why.

His parents had made their choice. And he would forever be grateful for the life and love they'd given to him and Alfred.

But he could not marry Persephone.

He could not subject her to the scorn she would face if she married the most unmarriageable man in London. Unmarriageable not because of his rakish ways. No, the *ton* loved a reformed rake. Unmarriageable because of his heritage. His mother. The language that felt as natural to him as English.

Another woman, a woman he did not love, maybe he could have managed it.

But not Persephone.

He could not be the source of her pain. And he could not watch her walk away, once she realized that he was not worth the persecution.

Edward carefully disentangled his leg, then slid his arm free and carefully set her head on the cushion. He righted his clothing. Gently tugged down her skirts so that her leg was no longer exposed.

Regret—that was what speared through him. He wished he'd lit every candle in his warehouse apartment when he'd had the chance. That he'd peeled off every layer of her clothing, worshiped her naked body for every second that was gifted to them.

He'd carry that regret with him.

But at least this way, she had a chance to be happy. To find the husband and have the family she desired. Persephone deserved it. She deserved the world.

He stood over her for several long moments, unable to go, knowing he could not stay.

Persephone's eyes remained closed. But he could see by the ragged rise and fall of her chest that she was not asleep.

He pressed one last kiss to her forehead, begging those eyes to open. Begging them to stay closed. Begging God above for some sort of salvation from his breaking heart.

But none came, and Edward walked out of Persephone's life for the second time.

Chapter Twenty-Three

Persephone barely recalled the rest of the evening. She did not know how long she lay there in the hothouse, refusing to open her eyes and acknowledge that she was, indeed, alone.

At some point, she found the strength to sit up, to fix her clothing and her hair. But even so, it had taken Madison no more than a glance to know that something was amiss. She did not ask questions or cluck her tongue in disapproval. She merely wrapped her arm around her charge—her friend—and took her home. She tucked her into bed and sat with her until Persephone finally fell asleep.

But when Persephone woke, she was once again alone.

She contemplated staying in her bed.

It's what she'd done a decade ago, in a bitterly cold January just like this one, when Edward had jilted her for the first time.

But she was not the same young woman she had been.

She rose from the bed and called for a maid. Let herself be dressed and primped while she sipped hot tea with honey. Then she descended the stairs, as she would have any other day, to face the world.

Even if it was a world that was infinitely paler than the one she'd woken to the day before.

The dining room was empty, food laid out on the sideboard. Madison's stack of newssheets was nowhere to be seen, which meant her friend had already broken her fast for the day. Persephone forced herself to walk to the sideboard, to pick up a plate... but she could not bring herself to reach for one of the boiled eggs or the still steaming scones. The very sight of them made her stomach turn.

She did not want food. She wanted company.

She didn't want to be alone.

She found Madison in the library on the other side of the sprawling Warsham mansion.

Persephone had never ventured there. Knowing it was a favorite of Henry and Madison both, it had always seemed like an intrusion. But desperation guided her steps that morning, and when she finally found it, the library doors were thrown open in silent invitation.

Madison was ensconced in a leather chair so big it nearly swallowed her petite form, a fresh pot of tea on her left and a stack of half-devoured periodicals on her right.

She did not jump to her feet and throw her arms around Persephone. Nor did pity shine out of those keen eyes—a small mercy. Madison merely inclined her head toward the frost-edged windows, where a chaise embroidered in red velvet was positioned, a thick knit blanket tossed over the foot.

"That is my most favorite seat in the entire house. It is perfect for looking over the gardens, for watching the sunrise, or for taking a nap," Madison said.

None of those things sounded particularly appealing to Persephone, but she accepted the invitation in any case. She settled herself onto the chaise, drawing the blanket up over her lap even though the library was perfectly warm.

She let her eyes drift aimlessly around the room. The walls

were lined with books, of course. The column of shelves nearest the desk must hold household or estate accounts of some kind; the volumes were thinner and haphazardly shelved from frequent use. She could not help but make observations, her mind cataloging the information without really intending to. She was the Lady Fixer, after all.

There was another stack on the little table to Madison's right. Not newssheets. The shape and thickness were all wrong.

"You have quite the stack of correspondence," Persephone heard herself say.

Madison tensed. Ever so slowly, she lowered the Hampshire Chronicle to her lap. This time, when she looked at Persephone, she failed to keep the sorrow from her eyes.

"They are all for you."

Persephone's heart sank.

"Invitations, mostly. I expect the butler will start bringing up calling cards in a few hours." Once it was the appropriate hour for social calls. For gentlemen to come and pay court.

Edward's plan had worked.

Invitations to balls, musicales, soirees. Invitations for her specifically. An indication of a new status, a new desirability.

Callers would come. Her dance card would be filled. All of it, with one goal in mind—marriage.

Marriage to a suitable gentleman of the *ton*.

Marriage to someone other than Edward.

Persephone broke.

One tear. Another. Then a cascade of them that covered her face, blurred her vision, had her gasping for her next breath.

"Oh, my sweet." Madison was there in a flash, wrapping her arms fiercely around her. She enveloped her, a feat which should have been impossible for someone so diminutive in build. But what Madison lacked in stature, she made up for in heart.

"You do not have to speak about it. Not a word, if you do not want to. Just cry and cry and cry, for as long as you need," she soothed, stroking her hand over Persephone's hair.

And she did.

It felt like hours, even though that was impossible, as no one came to inquire about luncheon or to bedevil her with news of callers.

She cried until her throat was raw, her eyes burning, and her heart so thoroughly broken, she doubted she'd ever be able to fit the pieces back together.

"You can tell me," she said softly. "I will not think any less of you."

Persephone huffed a soundless laugh. "Is that your way of gently telling me you won't turn me out or write to my parents to tell them I am a fallen woman?"

Madison's smile only deepened. "I wish I'd had the forethought to bed my husband before joining him at the altar. It might have clarified a few things."

This time, Persephone's laugh was audible. Madison Warsham *was* a walking scandal, but she could not help but feel blessed to have found a place in her heart. It should have felt wrong to laugh, after wringing herself out so thoroughly. But Persephone had given up trying to control the onslaught of emotions.

She rested her head on Madison's shoulder, staring at the wall of books across from her until they ceased to be spines and words and leather, but rather a flowing wave of muddled colors.

"For so long afterward, I chose not to believe in love," Persephone finally said.

"Because of Edward."

"Because of both of us. We were young, and stupid, and wildly in love. If two people can love one another that much and still have it end so horribly, then I wanted no part in it." She exhaled through her nose, waiting for more tears. But she'd cried all she had—*for now.*

"I did not know love like that existed," she said quietly. "My mother and father were an arranged match. While I do believe the affection between them is genuine, it's never been anything like what I felt with Edward."

Madison continued silently stroking her hair, letting her speak without interruption.

"We were engaged." She nearly choked on the word. "Not publicly, of course. There were no banns read. But our families had agreed."

Persephone had not allowed herself to remember like this in ages. The burn of betrayal, of loss... that was always with her. But to sink into the memories, to recall the events one by one, it was different. More painful. More real.

"Then things began to change. It started small, at first. I received fewer invitations. My sister-in-law overheard a pointed comment. It was the Countess of Tillbury who finally gave me the cut direct at court.

"I was devastated. I had always enjoyed that world of privilege. I was so damn naïve. I thought that nothing could touch me, the daughter of a duke. I assumed that Edward would be protected by extension.

"Then there was an incident."

Persephone dragged in a breath. So similar—it was so similar to what had happened in that alley only a few nights before.

"They called him the most terrible things. And then they noticed me."

Madison's hand stilled. "Persephone, you do not have to tell me—"

"No. It is better that you understand. That I remember."

Her voice shook, but Persephone recalled the incident with startling detail, even all these years later. No one had tried to physically harm her or Edward, not that time. But the things they'd said, implied... so terribly brutal. So ugly.

"You were scared," Madison said softly.

"More scared than I'd ever felt in my life," Persephone agreed.

Her friend resumed the gentle stroking of her hair. "It is understandable that you broke things off. You were young, you wanted to protect yourself."

Persephone jolted back. "You do not understand. I was scared for Edward, not for myself. It was the first time I truly understood the depth of the prejudice he faced—still faces—on a daily basis."

She moved out of Madison's arms, needing to sit on her own. "I loved Edward. I love him still. No matter what has happened between us... I have come to accept that I will love him until my dying breath. I did not break things off because I was afraid for myself. I did not break things off at all." She exhaled a shaking breath. "Edward did."

Madison did not reach for her, somehow knowing that Persephone could not stand it just then. She folded her hands in her lap, settling herself onto the chaise. Offering steady comfort.

"I have been blessed with a love like that," Madison said quietly. "But I have never lost it. I cannot pretend to know the pain you endure or even to offer you true advice. All I have is this, my friend—love does not limit. It does not take away. If this love is not the one to last the rest of your days, it does not mean that another will not come for you when the time is right."

She did reach for her then, grasping Persephone's hands tightly. "If you must let this love go, then mourn it. Cry about. Curse it. But when you're ready, whether it be a month or another decade... let love find you again."

Persephone's eyes dropped from the bookcase where she'd been staring. Down over the thick Aubusson, to her own hands clasping the blanket to her like a shield.

Let love find you again.

Twice, she'd found love.

She was not sure she'd survive if it ever found her again.

Chapter Twenty-Four

For the second time in a week, Edward was roused from sleep by a persistent knock on the warehouse door. It was midafternoon. But it had been nearly dawn before he'd finally fallen asleep, the misery that insisted on keeping him company finally losing to exhaustion.

Who could it be? Perhaps his father had decided—

"Ma?"

She stared up at him—shorter by more than a foot—and yet somehow her assessing gaze made him feel small. Like always.

"It is cold, Edward. Invite me inside," she ordered.

He stuffed down the curse that rose to his lips, stepping aside to allow her entry. He locked the warehouse door behind her, then followed as she climbed the long staircase up to his apartment.

"Mā, what are you doing here?" he asked as he shut the door behind him.

She was busy raking her eyes over the room, noting the crumpled bedsheets, then raking those sharp eyes over him.

Her dark eyes narrowed. "Why do you look so surprised?"

She'd chosen not to comment on the fact that he'd been

sleeping in the middle of the afternoon. Which meant she had something much worse planned.

Edward tried not to cringe. But he did not bother trying to snap his impenetrable mask of aloofness into place. Around is mother it would be of absolutely no use.

"I do not usually see you... here." Hell, he was muddling things. It had to be the lack of sleep. Not the fact that it felt as if some vital limb had been severed since he left... *No. It was not that.*

"I am the reason you have any food at all in this sad excuse for a home." She accepted the chair he pulled out for her at the little table, spearing him with her sharp eyes. "I can go places without your father."

"I never said otherwise."

"Hmph." She folded her hands on the tabletop. "Are you going to offer me tea?"

Edward let his mother wait in silence as he heated the water and added the fragrant green Camelia tea from the tin on the shelf. Only with his back to her did he allow himself to scrub his hand over his face. He hadn't meant to sleep all day. He needed to get back to work—to fill his mind with something other than his own misfortune. Once his mother left, he'd walk down to the dockside, where the offices of Johns Maritime Enterprises were located.

But that meant he had to deal with his mother first.

"Why are you here, Ma?" he asked as he offered her the tea kettle.

She poured for them both, taking a long sip before replying. "I am here to find out when you plan on making me a grandmother."

If the tea had been in his mouth, he surely would have choked on it.

"Surely Alfred is the more likely proposition in that regard," he managed.

His mother had been haranguing him for years to marry. Ever since Persephone left for America. He clamped down hard on that thought with the vice of his mind.

He'd always deferred her to Alfred. For once, it seemed like his brother was actually making progress on that front.

"He hardly lets his young lady out of his sight. You, meanwhile..." Eugenia's eyes swept around his apartment again as if she might find Persephone hiding in the corner. "I do not see Persephone anywhere. Despite what Mrs. Tso whispered in the grocery."

Confirmation.

She'd as good as given it to him in the boarding house, but there it was, irrefutable fact.

Edward had no desire to lie to his mother. But he also was not going to give her false hope.

"Persephone came to my aid in finding Alfred. We were stranded here overnight. That is what Mrs. Tso saw."

She set down the tea, having taken no more than that first sip. "If this had happened in Mayfair, the banns would be posted by now. Or her father would be riding to Canterbury to obtain a special license."

"The Duke and Duchess are on the continent."

"Which accounts for the fact that Persephone spent a night with you and no one was the wiser," she said sharply. There was no illusion of having tea left. This was an inquisition, and his mother was just getting started. "Just because I am not a member of the *ton*, does not mean I am unaware of how they function."

"There is nothing between me and Persephone." *Truth.* He hated those words.

"Horseshit."

Edward nearly fell out of his chair. He'd never heard his mother curse. Not in English, at least. "Ma—"

"Don't you dare scold me," she warned, jabbing him in the chest. "You are in love with that woman. Ten years, you've wasted sulking and longing for her. Now here she is again, as in love with you as you are with her. Yet your brother, the one who pretended to be kidnapped, is the one grinning while you glower at me over your tea."

"You do not understand." A stupid, untrue statement.

He knew he was going to tell her. For all that Edward looked up to his father, worshipped him, learned to run a business and be a man, his mother had always been the keeper of his heart. The one who'd soothed him when the other boys called him names. She'd cleaned his wounds from his first fist-fight.

He leaned forward on the table, his own tea abandoned now as well, bracing his forehead in his palms.

"You ought to understand," he said woodenly.

She lifted her eyebrows expectantly, but her voice was softer, if only a smidgen. "What ought I understand, my son?"

Edward thought for a long time about what to say. Long enough that the tea was no longer steaming beside them, long forgotten. He did not want to hurt her, to blame her. He was proud of his mother, of the man she'd shaped him into and the heritage she'd blessed him with. Hurting her would be nearly as bad as hurting Persephone.

"Loving Bà... it cannot have been easy," he finally said.

To his shock, she reeled back, laughing. "That is where you are entirely wrong, my son. Loving your father has been the easiest and most fulfilling thing I have ever done. Besides you and your brother, of course," she winked.

Edward blinked, struggling to comprehend... to make sense of the strange mixture of lightness and seriousness in her tone.

When he could not find the words, she continued.

"The world will do as it wishes. It is a different world now than it was when I first arrived in this country. There was no Limehouse, no place I could walk on the street and feel safe." Which explained why once Limehouse did grow up, it had become her safe haven. Perhaps it was not that she felt she couldn't leave Limehouse; but rather, she simply did not want to.

"It will undoubtedly change by the time you counsel your own children," she continued. A soft sigh. "Do not let life make your love hard."

Edward lifted his head enough to stare up at her from between his parted fingers. "What would you have me do?"

"Stop being an arse before I remove my shoe and beat you with it, as I had to when you were a thick-headed child." She shifted her weight as if she might actually do it. "You cannot know what Persephone will choose unless you let her make the choice. You decided for her all those years ago. She is a woman grown, Edward. She knows the way of the world. Give her the respect of making her own choice, choosing her own path. Choosing you."

"Mā," Edward said, his voice as small as a child's.

The hard line of her mouth did not soften. But her dark, wise eyes did. "What are you really afraid of, Edward?"

"That someday, she will realize her mistake." His gut wrenched at the words.

His entire life had been predicated on not taking a risk unless his chance of success was real and tangible. But Persephone... loving her was not the risk. It was trusting her to love him back. To expose himself to rejection, when he'd spent an entire life dodging it.

His mother leaned across the table, nudging away his hands, and took his face in her own. And he did feel every bit as small as he had when he was a child.

"You and Persephone have already made your mistakes. Consider yourselves lucky. Most of us fall headfirst in love and make the mistakes later. You two have managed to get it out of the way. Now let yourself have the love."

Chapter Twenty-Five

The amount of cosmetics it had taken to conceal the redness around her eyes was almost comical. Three days of endless crying. Madison had managed to stuff some food down her, to convince her to take nips of brandy here and there in hopes they would steady her. But Persephone had lived through this devastation before. She knew the only real medicine was time.

So, on the first day of February, she rose from her bed, concealed her agony with layers of powder, and put a white rose in her hair.

She'd turned away all callers. Let Madison respond to the invitations. Maybe her friend was right, and in a year or five she might be open to a new love. But the idea of dancing with another man, of letting someone other than Edward touch her, even for a brief, proper interaction... the thought made her skin turn icy.

It was not any husband, any family she wanted. It was Edward.

She would not torture herself with a placid comparison.

But she would still be the Lady Fixer of London.

"I believe my sister is seeking to disinherit me! Our poor

father, he is guileless in his old age," Lady Morley explained in a rapid whisper. She'd approached Persephone five minutes before, a glass of punch clutched in each hand and guarded hope in her eyes.

"Has she taken any concrete actions which lead you to believe such a thing?" Persephone asked. She tilted her head to the side as she listened, carefully tucking away the details the other woman shared, her fingers already beginning to itch for quill pen and notebook.

Lady Morley was the second person to approach her that evening, and the first set had only just begun.

At least she'd succeeded at one of her endeavors.

She felt him in the heartbeat before he spoke, some part of her body recognizing the change in temperature, the scent, the presence.

"Excuse me, is this dance taken?" Edward's voice rolled over her, a caress and a dagger to her soul.

"I do not dance tonight." She turned her back to him, giving her full attention to Lady Morley. She opened her mouth to tell the woman that she would accept the task and—

"A pity. I plan to," the blasted man said as he dragged her —*dragged her!*—onto the dance floor.

He managed not to step on her feet, but she would not do him the same courtesy. She slammed one heel down on his foot as they twirled. And the blasted arse did not flinch even an inch.

"Why are you here, Edward?" Persephone hissed, pretending that his fingers were not burning brands onto her skin, that her heart was not beating his name. *Ed-ward, Ed-ward, Ed-ward.*

"I promised you three social events," he said, then stepped away from her as the music dictated.

She could have used the moment to flee, but she did not dare leave this thing between them, this painful, gaping wound, open any longer.

"I rescind our agreement. You are free of me," she hissed as they came back together.

Edward caught her waist and held on tight. "*No.*"

"No?" She wrenched out of his arms, away from the other guests dancing, knowing she was making a scene but powerless to stop it. "What the hell do you mean by that?"

He caught her wrist. Held tight. Slowed her enough that she allowed him to tuck her hand into his arm. They looked like they were having a lover's quarrel.

It was painfully close to the truth.

She'd asked, but she did not really want to hear the answer to her question. She would let him lead her to the edge of the dance floor and then she would flee. She would hide in the ladies' retiring room for the rest of the night until Madison found her.

Not a good plan. But as good as she could be expected to come up with, given everything else.

Nowhere in that plan did she account for Edward stopping just on the threshold between the ballroom and the hall, lifting that hand from his arm, and brushing her knuckles against his lips.

"I am not free of you, Persephone," he murmured against her fingertips. "In fact, I do not think I have been free of you for a single day, a single breath, these last ten years."

"I have made so many mistakes. Pushing you away all those years ago. Misleading you about Alfred so that I might spend more time with you, convince you that I had changed. Only to hurt you again when I decided it was too dangerous. But it is not my decision to make. It is yours. I belong to you, Xīngān. I am so sorry for the pain that I have caused you, again and again. If you forgive me, if you let me love you, I will spend every day worshipping at your feet and giving you the love you deserve."

Her throat tightened painfully.

"Edward. Do not say these things."

His dark eyes met hers, thick with emotion he did not try to hide. "Why? Are you tempted to say them back?"

"Edward, please." She was going to break into a thousand pieces, right there on the parquet floors.

But Edward did not heed her plea. He lifted her knuckles to his face, dragged them down the strong line of his jaw, let his eyes flicker closed at the feel of her touching him, before he continued.

"Are you afraid that if I say I love you, that I have always loved you, that I will love you until the day I die... are you afraid you will want to say it back?"

The first tear fell.

"Because I do. And I have. And I will."

Another. So many tears, when she thought she'd cried them all.

"This is not fair," she said, biting hard into her lower lip.

There might have been a thousand eyes upon them, the entire *ton* watching as the notorious rake, the societal outcast, professed his love without a single care to who watched. But his words were soft, just for her, as he asked, "Do you love me, Persephone?"

She had only one answer for him, only the truth.

"Yes."

His eyes closed. By feeling alone, he pressed his lips to the soft mound of skin at the base of her thumb. The Mount of Venus.

When his eyes opened again, they were full of questions and worry. Fear and vulnerability. A man who had spent a lifetime learning to arm himself against the world, to be impervious to their jabs, laid himself bare before her with that one shared look.

"Will you ever..." he trailed off.

This time, he did not lift her hand. She lifted it herself, cupping his cheek. "I will never change my mind. I have not stopped loving you in ten years. I will not stop in a hundred. My love is constant and infinite and entirely for you. It has always been you."

The breath shuddered out of him. "Will you marry me?"

An unhinged giggle bubbled out of Persephone's chest. "Yes."

"Make a family together?"

The tears had slowed, but that started them anew.

"Yes," she managed.

Edward dragged his gaze away from her long enough to survey the crowded ballroom, the other guests pretending to not be watching them. Among them, Persephone spotted Madison and Henry. The former holding her husband's arm very tightly, likely to keep him from intervening.

"Leave with me right now?" Edward said when his eyes finally made their way back to her.

She cringed in the direction of Henry and Madison. "My chaperones might have something to say about it."

When she looked up into his eyes, the rake was there again. Her rake, from now until forever. "Shall we start our engagement with a scandal?"

"We might as well," she said breathlessly. "I am betrothed to the most unmarriageable man in London, after all."

She twined their fingers together, and without a backward glance, walked hand in hand with Edward to a future she'd spent more than ten years waiting for, only to find it sweeter than she'd ever imagined.

Neither of them noticed the tall woman lingering near the doorway, sipping her punch. She was unremarkable with her tight chignon and downcast eyes. Of course, people rarely noticed the Brazen Belle.

Epilogue

Limehouse, London
January 1825

They really ought to be sleeping. It had been nearly three years since they'd had a silent, uninterrupted night alone in their own bed.

But as night fell, steadily casting their bedroom in starlight, neither of them closed their eyes. At least, not to sleep.

Persephone pressed hers tightly shut as she arched off the bed, Edward's fingers stroking deeper inside of her with every thrust.

"Stop teasing," she moaned. She did not try to modulate her volume. For once, they were blessedly alone.

"You've become so demanding, Mrs. Johns," Edward murmured against her.

"I am a woman who knows what she wants in the little time she has," she gasped out, pushing up onto her elbows and opening her eyes so she could watch him pumping his hand inside of her.

He did not slow the pace, even as his eyes drifted up to meet hers, a smirk stealing over his handsome face.

"We have all night," he growled softly.

Persephone recognized the predatory intent in his eyes a second before he dipped down to truly torture her. He flicked his tongue over her center of pleasure.

"Edward," she cried. "Edward, oh please, oh my love."

He stroked her faster, his tongue driving over that sensitive spot again and again while he curled his fingers inside of her. She reached down, sliding her fingers into his silky hair and holding his mouth tight against her cunt in silent demand. Persephone felt him chuckle against her dark curls, and tried to swat him. But a second later she ceased to care.

She plummeted over the edge, her climax claiming her body and all rational thought.

Her legs shook as Edward slowly drew away. One hand caressed her inner thigh, then her hip, stroking her softly as the shaking throes of need ebbed away.

He caught her eye. Held her gaze as he lifted his other hand—the one drenched in her juices—to his lips and sucked his fingers into his mouth.

Just like that she was shaking again.

Once he'd sucked away all of her nectar from his fingers, he dropped them to her body. He caressed the soft expanses of skin as he made his way up from between her legs to her mouth.

His fingers grazed reverently over the white marks on her abdomen, where her body had stretched and changed to carry their precious children. Cherubic three-year-old twin girls who on that particular evening were ensconced two houses down with their năi nai, Eugenia.

Finally, he stretched out above her, covering her body with his and dragging his fingertips over her lips.

Persephone sucked them into her mouth, nibbling, savoring the faint taste of her pleasure that lingered there mixed with the scents of bergamot and anise that were so purely Edward.

"You are trembling," Edward observed, smiling lazily.

"Whose fault is that," she laughed, burying her face in his shoulder.

For a moment, with the waves of her peak still rolling through her body, it was almost too much. The comfortable, richly appointed bedroom where they lay together, in the house they'd built on the same Limehouse street as Edward's family. Knowing their children were safe and loved, still close enough she could go to them if she wanted. Being there with Edward, the only person she'd ever wanted to share her life with... it was perfection. It was so much more than she'd ever dared to hope, five years ago or fifteen.

"I love you," Persephone breathed into Edward's neck, fighting back the tears.

He shifted his weight so that he was beside her rather than above, somehow managing not to dislodge her from where she clung to him.

Persephone let out a quivering breath at the friction of their bodies moving against one another. But Edward tangled his fingers in her hair, twining her curls around his hand so he could tilt her head back just enough to whisper in her ear.

"I love you, Xīngān. Thank you for choosing me."

Her heart filled to nearly bursting as she tipped her head back to kiss him. "I always will."

* * *

Are you wondering about Persephone's scandalous hosts, Madison and Henry? Their story is the first book in my Hesitant Husbands series. Looking for even more steam? Little Nora Warsham is all grown up and ready to find true love in **The Duchess Who Dared**, the first in an all new historical romance series from Cara Maxwell.

Coming Soon: Book 2 in The Rake Review, *The Fake February Rake* **by Charlie Lane**

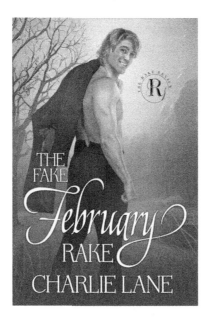

The ton thinks Hades is a rake. He's not.

Before the Brazen Belle's gossip column named him February's rake, Dr. Hades Jones was the ton's most trusted doctor, proper in every way but for his family's scandalous past. But the rake the Belle named wasn't him. It was someone wearing his distinctive silk-lined coat, which was stolen from him months ago. Now Hades is on the hunt for the coat thief, and what he finds in a Covent Garden alley is not what he expects—a woman with doe eyes, a steel spine, and a tart tongue he unexpectedly wants to taste.

Everyone thinks she's Hades. She's just wearing his coat.

Lady Ophelia Howard has one purpose in life—protect the women of London from rakes, scoundrels, and rogues. Unable to save her father's mistress, she'll do whatever she must to keep other women from suffering the same fate, including theft. She stole the devilishly handsome doctor's coat to hide her identity while sneaking women to safety. She didn't mean to smear his good name.

And now he's caught her, and he insists she help restore his reputation. Any way she can. Including marriage. But can marriage to an earl's daughter bring the ton calling once more? Or will Ophelia's radical secrets ruin them both?

Also by Cara Maxwell

HESITANT HUSBANDS

Lady Leonora Knows Best

A Love Match for the Marquess

Meant to be Mine

Love Once Lost

A Very Viscount Christmas

* * *

RACING ROGUES

Rogue Awakening

One Rake to Ruin

The Speed of Seduction

To Please a Princess

The Secret of the Surviving Earl

Riding with a Rake

First Lady to the Finish

* * *

LADY KNIGHTS

Author's Note

I don't think I have ever had such a packed Author's Note, but there were so many little details I included in this book which I wanted readers to be able to reference. So here we go!

Though we typically think of the London social season beginning later in spring, it did generally correspond with the sitting of Parliament. The years 1819 and 1820 were tumultuous in England, from the Peterloo Massacre all the way through the death of George III, the trial of Caroline of Brunswick, and beyond. There were multiple special sessions of Parliament convened, including one from November 1819 through February 1820. Which means in January 1820, where our story takes place, the who's who of English society would have been in London.

I reference the Peterloo Massacre only briefly in the book. However, it is a real event that stemmed from the economic slump in England after the Napoleonic Wars (among other complicating events). I won't go into detail here since it isn't truly relevant to Edward and Persephone's story, but it's a fascinating bit of history to look into, especially for the contrast it provides to our commonly held notions of the romance of the Regency era.

A couple of years ago, while researching a different book, I came across an interesting historical note about a group of Chinese women who became stranded in England in the 1800s, some of whom went on to marry Englishmen and settle in England permanently. I spent *hours* trying to find this original article, as it was the source of my inspiration for Edward's family. In the process of not finding it, I did find so much other rich historical information about Chinese immigration to England in the nineteenth century.

Chinese immigrants were very much a part of the vibrant history of London in the 1800s, particularly along the River Thames. John Anthony was the first Chinese immigrant to gain British Citizenship, which he did in 1805 after building a lucrative career with the East India Company. Limehouse, the riverside community where Edward and Persephone eventually make their home, was London's first Chinatown. Though in 1820 Limehouse was only just beginning to take shape, I like to imagine Edward and Persephone investing money and raising their family where their language and heritage would be celebrated. So I fudged the dates a bit—anything in the service of a happy ending, right?

Though I refer to the language spoken by Edward and his family as "Chinese" because that is how they would have referred to it, they would most likely have spoken some variation of Mandarin. I included several Mandarin words throughout the book, in their Romanized/Pinyin form (Pinyin is the western standard system for transliterating Chinese characters). However, I also wanted to include them in their authentic form for readers to reference, so below you will find those terms in Mandarin Chinese characters, Pinyin, and their approximate meaning in English.

心肝 Xīngān = darling
奶奶 nǎi nai = paternal grandmother
爸爸 Bàba (Bà) = informal father
妈妈 Māmā (Mā) = informal mother

Writing Edward and Persephone's story was a challenge, but ultimately a joy. I hope that readers love them as much as I have.

About the Author

Bringing fresh perspective and punch to the genre readers already know and love, Cara Maxwell is dedicated to writing spirited heroines and irresistible rogues who you will root for every time. A lifetime reader of romance, Cara put pen to paper (or rather, fingers to keyboard) in 2019 and published her first book. She hasn't slowed down from there.

Cara is an avid traveler. As she explores new places, she imagines her characters walking hand-in-hand down a cobblestone path or sharing a passionate kiss in a secluded alcove. Cara is living out her own happily ever after in Seattle, Washington, where she resides with her husband, daughter, and two cats, RoseArt and Etch-a-Sketch.

—

Printed in Great Britain
by Amazon